DANCING THROUGH LIFE
BOOK FIVE

DELICIOUS Secrets

PATRICIA M. ROBERTSON

Chapter 1

Some secrets are so delicious you just have to keep them to yourself. Like chocolate on a hot summer day, they melt in your mouth. You want to hold them for as long as possible, never giving way to the need to swallow. Their sweetness bursts with flavor. To swallow would be to lose them forever and so you hold on for as long as possible, relishing every morsel.

Other secrets are too good to keep to yourself. They beg to be shared, taunting you, "tell me, tell me!"

And others are meant to be kept silent. They crawl into the recesses of the mind where, if you are lucky, you forget they even exist. There are secrets that in telling cause unnecessary harm. Better to keep silent.

And then there are those that need to be told to clear the air. You have to fight to hold them in. You want to spit them out lest they contaminate the good. You hope that in the sharing they will be robbed of their power.

A family is as healthy as its secrets. I guess the same can be said about a community.

I'm an expert on secrets so I ought to know. I am the holder of the key to multiple secrets, the gatekeeper of secrets. I'm a secretary!

"Is the Sunday bulletin ready, Marcie?" Pastor Joe stood at her desk, Marcie quickly shut the file she was working on.

"Sure, Pastor, ready to go," she said.

"Good. Would you send it to me so I can proof it before we run copies?"

"Sure, only ..."

"Only what?"

"I've got that thing."

"What thing?"

"You know, that thing. I told you about it last week. Don't you remember?"

"Could you help me out?"

"What good is telling you anything if you are just going to forget? I'll be back by noon. You'll have your bulletin then." Marcie closed her computer and prepared to leave.

"All right. Just make sure I have it on my desk when I return from lunch."

"I'll work through my lunch hour to do it," Marcie reassured him as she picked up her laptop and left. That would buy her some time, she thought. She loved how easy it was to get over on her boss. The fact that he was a minister made it all that much simpler. She would go to the local coffee shop, order a latte and finish her work in the cozy atmosphere. So much more fun than the boring church office.

Joe wondered about his new church secretary. Something just wasn't right, but he couldn't put his finger on it. Is it possible he was being played?

Ever since Edna, the previous secretary had retired, he had been struggling to find her replacement. No one wanted to work for the wages the church could afford. And at thirty hours a week, the church didn't include benefits.

The minute he thought he had a replacement, they would leave for a full-time position with benefits, something he just couldn't provide.

"Sorry, Pastor, I need the hours and benefits," they would explain as they cleared their desk.

"I understand," he said, and he did. The position required someone who considered it a calling, someone who didn't need to support themselves or their family. Someone who didn't need the money. It required a special someone. Someone who knew how to keep him organized, who was discreet, who could be trusted with confidential information. Edna had been that special someone. He wouldn't find anyone like her. At this point he would appreciate anyone with computer skills who actually showed up. He had even tried his daughter, Michelle, in the position, but between school and all of her senior activities, she just couldn't put in the hours he needed.

Marcie was a church member's daughter. He had agreed to give her a shot at the position as a favor to her father. She had dropped out of college and ended up back on her dad's doorstep.

"Give her a chance, Pastor. She just needs to get some direction." Joe had agreed despite his concerns. He didn't want to be the place where wayward young adults got their footing before taking off. He wanted someone he could rely on for the long haul. He didn't want to have to keep training new secretaries. It took time he didn't have, time away from his ministry. He had reluctantly agreed.

"So, how's the latest secretary shaping up?" Kathleen had asked him over for dinner that night. He and Kathleen had been dating off and on for the past year. They had both wanted to keep the relationship quiet, as secret as possible for someone living in the fishbowl of a pastorate. Rather than going out in public, they took turns having each other over for dinner, where they could talk in the relative quiet of their homes, that is, if you didn't count family members coming and going.

"I don't know. There's something not quite right."

"I saw her at the coffee shop this morning, chatting with her friends."

"So that's the thing."

"What thing?"

"Never mind. So, she was playing hooky from work."

"She did have her laptop with her. She was working on something."

"Not church work, I'm sure." She had done a good job on the bulletin though, when he finally got it that afternoon. When she did work she could get a lot done at once. She was efficient.

"Maybe she just needs some direction." Kathleen twirled the spaghetti on her fork.

"That's what her dad says, but this isn't career counseling. I need someone I can count on."

"But it is a church." Joe was aware that Kathleen knew something about needing direction. She had been one such young person. Her misdirection had landed her in prison. "You know, if Joy hadn't taken interest in me, I wouldn't be here." Joy, her sister-in-law, had seen the potential in Kathleen when she had returned home after her jail stint. She had believed in her, given her a chance, given her purpose, direction. Joy had died from breast cancer several years ago. Now

Kathleen was in charge of the Arts Center named after Joy, giving her ample opportunity to work with other directionless young people.

"Yes, well, I have enough young people needing direction in the youth group. I don't need another one in my office. If she needs direction, let her get involved with the young adults at church, not play at secretary."

"You know it doesn't always work that way," Kathleen reminded him.

Joe knew. He couldn't argue the point.

"As you always say, God works in strange ways. Who knows why God placed this young woman under your care," Kathleen continued.

Joe had said similar things to Kathleen over the past years. "Touché. Now I see how patronizing those words sound. You've made your point."

"That wasn't my point, however ..." Kathleen smiled as she sipped her after dinner coffee.

Chapter 2

"Hey, Marcie," the two young women tapped her on her headphones and sat down. "What're you doing?"

"Hey," Marcie took off her headphones and paused the program on her computer. "I'm listening to a webinar on the 'laptop life' – making money through the internet."

"Let me tell you how it ends," Gwen started. "Sign up for my on-line course and I'll teach you in ten easy lessons how you can do your own on-line course and make money off of losers like you."

"That pretty much sums it up." Marcie took a sip from her coffee, savoring the aroma. "But you can get some useful information from these free seminars before the sales pitch breaks in. I usually exit at that point."

"So, is that your latest get rich quick scheme?" Maya teased.

"Pretty much," Marcie teased back.

"No, tell us. What is it you are up to, all the time typing away at your computer?" Maya asked. "We know you. You're always up to something."

"Okay, if you promise not to tell anyone." Maya and Gwen put their fingers to their mouths to indicate their silence. "I'm writing a book."

"What about?" Gwen asked.

"That's it. It's a secret," Marcie said.

"What secret?" Gwen asked.

"I'm not sure just yet. I'm digging around. This town is full of secrets." Marcie's eyes glimmered as she spoke about secrets.

"Yeah, right." Maya dismissed Marcie's statement.

"No, it is. You have to open your eyes, look around and keep your ears open. St. Luke's is the perfect place to hear secrets."

"Speaking of St. Luke's, aren't you supposed to be working?" Gwen asked.

"Oh, Pastor Joe is so easy to get over on. He'd believe me if I told him the pope was on line one," Marcie explained.

"Lying to a pastor?" Gwen continued.

"Just stretching the truth a little. What he doesn't know won't hurt him."

"I don't know about that," Maya said. "Isn't there a special place in hell for liars, especially those who lie to ministers?"

"I think that applies to ministers who lie and lead their sheep astray. They are held to a 'higher' standard. That's why this book will be so great."

"You mean you're writing about Pastor Joe?" Gwen asked.

"You know there's more there than meets the eye. First there's that woman he's dating. What's up with that?" Marcie leaned in and lowered her voice. "From what I heard she not only doesn't attend St. Luke's, she doesn't attend any church. And rumor has it that she smoked pot in the church's woman's lounge."

"Maybe the novel should be about her," Gwen suggested.

"Oh, no, Pastor Joe's the greater mystery. I just have to figure it out. And this whole town. It's full of secrets and I'm in the best place to learn them as a church secretary." Marcie had long thought that there were mysteries all around if you are open to it. She remembered being in grade school and riding her bike past the old Victorian house on the corner of First and Michigan and imagining that it was haunted.

"Oh, the secrets those walls could tell," she had said to herself. There had to be hidden passageways somewhere in the recesses of the house, hidden cubby holes, spaces under stairs to hide. They were ripe to be found by the right person, and she was that person. As a child she had made several attempts at writing a mystery novel set in the home, then gave it up for more interesting pursuits once she had entered Middle School. Still, the conviction had remained that there were secrets everywhere, waiting for her to discover them, even in boring old Cascade Falls. That would be her ticket out. She would write her novel, make her fortune and be gone.

"Then what are you doing here?" Gwen asked.

"I was just going to ask that myself," a male voice interrupted.

"Pastor Joe," Maya said. She and Gwen jumped up.

"We were just leaving," Gwen said, abandoning Marcie to the consequences of her actions. Call me, Gwen gestured with her hand as she left.

"I'm not paying you to drink coffee and talk to your friends," Joe continued.

"But there's nothing to do. I have all my work done. Wouldn't you rather I drink coffee here and pay for it with my own money then drink the church's coffee?"

"Someone has to be in the office to answer the phone and the door. I thought I had made that clear when I hired you."

"Yes, Pastor," Marcie feigned meekness. "Can I go now?"

"As long as you are going back to the church."

"Yes, Pastor," Marcie said again. She flipped her laptop shut and stood up. "You know, you should think about getting a Keurig or an espresso maker. I don't know how you can drink that dishwater you call coffee." Marcie stopped to get a refill. She glanced in Pastor Joe's direction and saw him shake his head as he watched her leave.

Chapter 3

Delicious Secrets
From the Desk of Sally Sweetstuff
Church of St. Everybody
Pastor I. M. Knowitall

Pastor Knowitall, or Pastor K, of the church of St. Everybody had another busy day today. The buxom brunette temptress was seen leaving his office at 9 a.m., after an early morning appointment.

"Ms. Sweetstuff," Pastor K tucked in his shirt as he approached. What's my first appointment for the day?"

"I believe you just had it with Ms. Blossom."

"After that one. What's my next appointment?"

"Why Mrs. Mandelbaum to talk about the funds for the orphans."

"Yes, that's right. Our biggest donor. Be sure to let me know as soon as she arrives. Mustn't make Mrs. MoneyBags, er Mandelbaum, wait." Pastor K adjusted his tie.

"No, Pastor. Of course not." I buzzed his office when Mrs. Mandelbaum arrived.

"Mrs. MoneyBags, er Mandelbaum, is here Pastor. Should I send her in?"

"I'll be right out." Pastor K came out, making sure his suit jacket was properly fit about his lean frame. He extended his hand to Mrs. Mandelbaum. "So good to see you, Harriet."

"I hope you still think so after what I have to tell you. Mind you, I'm not one to tell tales."

"Of course not," Pastor said as he led her into his office.

"But everyone is coming to me about this ..." I heard until Pastor K shut the door to his office.

What was it this time? Was it the boys chewing gum in church again? Or the babies crying during her solo? Or perhaps someone had been smoking pot in the ladies' restroom again?

Stay tuned to find out.

SS

Marcie couldn't believe how boring the church office was, despite what she had told her friends. She had been faking it so her friends wouldn't know what a loser she was. The job at the church had been her dad's idea, not hers. She was trying to make the best of it.

She was serious about writing a book. She had to do something to justify her existence in her own mind. And besides, there was good money in it if you know what you are doing, at least that was what all the webinars she was attending and podcasts she was listening to told her. Problem was, she had yet to write more than five hundred words. That wouldn't get her anywhere. She had to start writing every day, she told herself, but then she saw another webinar on marketing and yet another article on writing and self-publishing and she was down another rabbit hole, following leads that got her nowhere. So she decided to start blogging.

She knew she was right about secrets; she just wasn't as privy to them as she had led her friends to believe.

"Make them up," a voice in her head told her. "It's fiction, after all."

"Yes, but you're supposed to write what you know," another voice told her. She didn't know which voice to believe, so she chased after another idea down a hole and got lost where it was warm and comfortable.

She didn't regret dropping out of college. Senior year. Only a year to go, her dad had told her.

"Certainly you can hang in there for one more year," he had said.

"No, I can't," Marcie had replied.

What her father didn't know was that Marcie had more than one year left to complete her degree, thanks to switching majors three times over the past three years. She didn't know what she wanted to do. What was the use of continuing and getting a degree if you don't know what you want to do? If she was wasting her time, wasn't it better to do that at home, rather than pile up student loans? As it was, it would take her at least a year and a half if not two years to complete her degree, a degree in a field that no longer interested her.

Her dad had okayed her coming home as long as she got a job and paid her expenses.

"I'm telling you, time for you to start taking more responsibility, young lady," her dad had said.

"Yeah, yeah, yeah," Marcie had slapped her headphones back on and gone to her room. She was surprised when her father didn't follow her, pull the head phones off, and insist that they talk. Perhaps he was giving her some time. Or perhaps he was counting on Pastor Joe to work his "magic" on her. Whatever the reason, she realized she was stuck.

And so, she had ended up working as a secretary at her home church, a dead-end job in a dead-end town.

Chapter 4

There's a parade of characters each week, each one with a story to tell ... Each one with a secret ... Marcie made up these secrets. What surprised her was that she was starting to get a following. Not just people in Cascade Falls, but people throughout the country and other countries, other continents. She didn't know how they stumbled upon her blog, but they did. She made sure she had a funny picture to go with each blog post then posted it on Instagram to reach more people. What's more, she started to get comments on her posts. Just one or two at first, then as many as twenty or thirty as her followers grew. And many of them thought she was writing about their church or a church in their town.

It seemed there were more similarities across churches than she had imagined. She called her church St. Everyone. The town, Cascades. The Pastor was Reverend Ivan Michael Knowitall, because, after all, aren't all pastors know-it-alls, the repositories of all knowledge, or at least so they thought. Punctilious pundits who proclaimed proofs from their pulpit, Marcie thought with a chuckle and added the phrase to her blog.

She painted herself in a much more flattering manner. She was Sally Sweet, who smiled and lowered her horned-rimmed glasses when people approached her, seeking her homespun wisdom. She experimented with the name, rolling it around in her mind to see if she liked it. She gave herself wisdom beyond her years. She had considered aging herself to a stereotypical grandmotherly type, more befitting her august role as sage secretary, then decided against it because she didn't know whether she could pull it off. No, better to be her own age, although not specific about it. It would be her secret. She would be so sweet that maple syrup would ooze from her pores. Oooh, she liked that reference. Now how to use it in her blog?

Yes, sugar didn't begin to encompass how sweet she was, Sally Sweet. Or Sally Sweetstuff. She liked that better. She started signing off each post with SS.

Chapter 5

Delicious Secrets – The Mysterious Fast Eddie

Legends abound around Eddie. Fast Eddie, some called him. Others, Fearless Eddie. Still others, Frenetic Eddie. He's a fixture not just at church functions, but around town. He doesn't own a car, yet he shows up at events and activities all over the county. He attends every funeral and wedding at the church and is a fixture at school reunions. Unsuspecting brides are surprised to see him popping up in their wedding pictures. He has been known to show up at a graduation open house in the afternoon, then a wedding reception across town for dinner and finally ending up at the Crab Shack on Otter Lake, all with no visible means of transportation.

Rumor has it that he is one of God's angels, checking up on the residents of Cascades, challenging them to show hospitality to this guest who shows up out of nowhere and is gone just as quickly. Others say he is a secret billionaire, hiding his money in the trailer he inhabits on the outskirts of town. Still others, that he lost his mental capacity during the seventies through drug experimentation, or that he was experiencing the after-effects of years as a prisoner of war during the Vietnam War.

And you? What about you? Who do you say he is? Send me your stories. The best will be included in my blog.

SS

"So, how goes the *secret* book?" Gwen asked, making quotes with her fingers.

"Oh, it goes," Marcie sighed.

"That bad?"

"No, not bad, just ..." Marcie searched for the right word. What could she say? "It just is." Try though she might, her writing was searching for a reason to exist. There was no meat to it. No substance. She wanted to write more than little anecdotes or made up gossip.

She watched as the Vietnamese girl in front of her carefully applied lacquer to her toes. Marcie thought of her as but a slip of a girl, hardly sixteen, though she figured she was closer to her own age. She was slight of build and never looked Marcie in the face, keeping her head lowered respectfully. Marcie's attempts at conversation were met with quiet. The woman who ran the shop ran interference, explaining, "She doesn't speak English." The shop owner was happy to keep up a running conversation in place of her "girls." She also intervened when Marcie tried to tip her.

"Tips into tip jar. All my girls share tips," she explained and pointed to the jar on the reception desk.

"Okay," Marcie gave up her attempt to engage the girl in conversation.

"I still can't believe how cheap these mani-pedis are," Marcie commented to Gwen as they left. "I'm used to paying three times this amount, besides the tip."

"I know. It's a great deal. At these rates, I can afford to come every week. I wonder how she does it," Gwen questioned.

"Who cares, just so she continues to do it rather than raising her rates."

The nail parlor was a small establishment with only two chairs for pedicures, four stations for manicures. Those chairs were kept busy. There were only three manicurists that Marcie could see. She was growing fond of her regular person, Mei-Lyn, or so the owner called her. She made a point of requesting her whenever she made an appointment. Mei-Lyn was new to the country. The other manicurists had more of a grasp of English, though they still talked rarely and then amongst themselves in Vietnamese.

She didn't like the owner. She was disingenuous, with her feigned solicitousness.

"It's their culture," Gwen had tried to explain. "They say yes even when they mean no in order to maintain the relationship."

"No, it's more than that. I just don't like her," Marcie insisted. The owner's son was even worse. He wasn't always there, but when he was he talked to the clients in ways that made her want to climb into the shower. It wasn't so much what he said, just the way he said it and the way he ogled the manicurists and touched them as if they had no right to their own bodies.

Marcie looked about the room, noting the tidy desk for signing in customers, scheduling appointments and checking out. The girls were dressed in trim, light-blue uniforms. Mei-Lyn's hair was neatly pulled back in a bun and covered by a scarf. The others had their hair done in differing fashions, shoulder length or pigtails, still pulled back by the same scarf. They talked to each other in a sing-song fashion, laughing at private jokes until reprimanded by the owner. Sometimes Mei-Lyn was the brunt of the jokes, Marcie noted while she and Gwen carried on their conversation.

"Want to do something this weekend?" Gwen said as they left the salon.

"Sure, what theme?" There really wasn't much going on in Cascade Falls, they had agreed long ago and so came up with their own entertainment.

"Bikers? We could wear tight jeans and leather jackets and ride our bikes downtown. Or maybe a Hawaiian theme. We could get mocktails at the Crab Shack." The Crab Shack, so called because of the crab races held there each summer, was a popular hang-out.

"Too cold outside," Marcie nixed the idea.

"How about preppy?"

"Nah, that's passé."

"French?"

"There are no French restaurants in town."

"Italian? We could get pizza? Or better yet, Japanese. We could dress up in kimonos and eat sushi." Gwen pretended to pull her short hair on top of her head as if in a bun and walked with tiny steps.

"Where would we get kimonos?"

"We could come up with something. We could wrap flowered sheets around us." Gwen demonstrated, wrapping an imaginary sheet around her body.

"Too much like a toga." Marcie nixed that idea as well.

"Then how about a toga? Or maybe we could do a zombie night?" Marcie and Gwen had been doing dress-up since they were children. Half the fun was coming up with ideas. Gwen's mother had started it by hosting Hawaiian afternoons in the dead of winter. She would turn up the heat, have them put on bathing suits, put a small wading pool in the living room and feed them pineapples and popsicles. The girls loved it. Marcie had quickly fallen in love with both Gwen and her mother.

Marcie had been delighted when she had met Gwen in first grade and discovered she lived only a block away. They had been fast friends ever since. Gwen's family had moved there when her dad, a physician, had been hired at the local hospital. She was the youngest of four, with two older brothers and one sister. Her brothers had been already in high school, her sister, six years older than her, was in seventh grade. Gwen was the beloved baby one minute, spoiled and fussed over, the next quickly forgotten as her siblings were pre-occupied with more important ventures than watching a little sister who wanted to tag-along. As such, Gwen sometimes felt alone in her family of six, everyone living in their own world, her dad with his busy practice, her siblings with their lives, and her mom ... well, her mom was also lost in her own drama where she was the central character. Gwen had been as grateful to find a friend and sister in Marcie as Marcie had been grateful to find Gwen.

Gwen's mom had been so full of life back then, lavishing attention on all four of her children, but especially on her youngest as the three oldest sought to break free into their own identities. There had been good days with the "fun" mom. Marcie used to love going over to Gwen's, being petted and fussed over as her mom's energy and affection seemed to overflow on to anyone in its path. She used to think that maybe here was a second family, the family she had always wanted, with two parents, older brothers to tease her and an older sister to imitate. Not that she didn't love her dad. It was just so quiet with no one to play with, only the housekeeper around while her dad was at work, and her dad home at night.

There had been tea parties with large floppy hats and pretty dresses – the hats and dresses provided by Gwen's mother who had a flair for the dramatic. Gwen's mom always called her Marcella instead of Marcie. Marcie would have resented it from anyone else, but from Mrs. Thompson, it was okay.

"Marcie is such a plain name. Marcella is so much better. So much more romantic. I dub thee Princess Marcella and Princess Gwendolyn." Mrs. Thompson tapped each of them on the head with a toy wand and gave them tiaras along with the title. What was there not to adore?

Marcie had loved dressing up in Gwen's mom's feather boas and flopping around in her high heels. There was no such female paraphernalia in her home. And sometimes Gwen's mom put her make-up on them. Those were good times.

But then there were those days when everything wasn't going as well, when Gwen couldn't have any friends over. When Gwen retreated to the outdoors in order to be away from her home or wanted to go to Marcie's home.

"It's so quiet here." Gwen sighed, luxuriating in the silence that was Marcie's home.

"Too quiet. Why can't we go to your house and play?"

"Because, like I told you, my mom has a headache. I can't have any friends over." Sometimes these headaches went on for weeks at a time. Marcie hadn't understood it back then.

By the time Gwen reached high school, all three of her siblings were long gone, off to college in other parts of the country, leaving Gwen as her mother's sole companion and caretaker as her dad spent long hours at work. Gwen didn't like to talk about it. Marcie remembered that day in her freshman year of high school. She had gone over to Gwen's when she hadn't received answers to her repeated calls. When no one answered her knock on the back door she had tried the door. Finding it unlocked, she had walked in. The house was silent. The only light in the kitchen came from the windows.

"Gwen?" Marcie had called quietly. She had jumped at the sound of her own voice in the empty room. She had walked into the darkened hallway and heard the sound of a TV coming from the front room. The room was dark except for the glow of the TV screen. The curtains were pulled shut.

"Gwen?" Marcie asked again. "Mrs. Thompson?" Gwen's mother seemed to be swallowed by the couch.

"What are you doing here?" Gwen stopped Marcie before she could go further into the room.

"You didn't answer my phone calls."

"Who's there?" Gwen's mother stirred on the couch.

"Marcie, Mom. Don't worry."

Mrs. Thompson slouched back down into the couch without a word as if the effort to speak had drained her of every bit of energy.

"Do you want anything, Mom?"

"No," the listless figure responded. Gwen took Marcie back to the kitchen.

"Is she always like this? Is it another headache?" Marcie asked.

"Yeah, sure, a headache. I'm sorry. I had my phone turned off so the noise wouldn't bother Mom. I can't come over."

"I see that. Is there anything I can do?"

"No, I just have to wait till she pulls out of this."

"How long will that be?"

"Don't know. She seems to be getting worse. Her bad days are lasting longer."

"I'm so sorry."

"Well, it is what it is." Gwen looked away. "You better go. I have to check on her."

Marcie had asked her dad about it that night. "Dad, do you know what's wrong with Gwen's mom?"

Henry had stopped eating and looked at her. "What do you know?"

"It's just I went over there today and she had all the curtains closed. It was eerie."

"Is Gwen okay?"

"I guess, but she said she had to take care of her mom. It was one of her headaches again."

"Gwen's mother isn't well." Marcie's dad shook his head and looked down. "Now that her sister is gone, Gwen must be the one taking care of her."

"But what is it? Is it cancer?" Cancer would be bad, but Marcie knew something about it from books she had read and movies. She had this romantic notion of helping Gwen take care of her mother, if only Gwen would let her in on the secret. They could be just like the characters she read about.

"No, it's not cancer." Marcie could see that her dad knew more than he was saying. Why all the secrecy?

"Then tell me," Marcie demanded.

"It's not for me to tell."

"You mean I have to ask Gwen?"

"Yes."

"But she doesn't want to talk to me about her mother."

"No, but maybe she needs to." Marcie started to ask her dad again when he told her to finish her meal and clear the table. "I've got some work to do in my study."

Marcie had learned not to press Gwen to tell her about her mom. It remained a secret pact between the two of them.

Marcie knew that was why Gwen hadn't gone away to college, instead attending the local community college then transferring to a Christian college nearby. It wasn't because of any great love for Cascade Falls. The agreement with her dad was that he would pay all her bills and give her spending money as long as she stayed home, went to a local college, and took care of her mom. He even provided her with a car and gas money. Gwen was free to come and go as she pleased as long as her mom was doing okay. On those occasions when her mom wasn't doing okay, Gwen would go to class then return home immediately. Even on her worst days her mom was all right alone for several hours, long enough for Gwen to run errands and go to class. Fortunately, she had been better this spring, allowing Gwen to go out with her friends and almost have a life of her own.

They finally decided on a movie night.

Chapter 6

Delicious Secrets

Mrs. Henderson (name changed to protect the guilty) wears her cockapoo on her shoulders like an oversized brooch. She comes to see Pastor K at least once a week. She doesn't have anything better to do, at least as far as I can tell. But I suspect she has a secret life. She wasn't always old and alone. She had a secret lover, many years ago, but her father didn't approve. She ran off with her lover but when he left her alone and pregnant, she returned home. Her father welcomed her back on one condition – that she give up any contact with her former lover, and relinquish the baby. The baby was given away in a concealed adoption. She never knew her little girl or the adoptive family. Instead she had a series of small dogs.

She stayed home with her father, inherited the family estate after he died and now continues his legacy of interfering with the affairs of the church. Money is power. I call her Mrs. Honeybucks. And so she uses this power to dictate the goings on in the church, but I know better. Under that icy exterior is a mother in search of her child. Maybe there is a grandchild waiting to find her grandmother, Marcie wrote on her laptop. No wait ... She deleted the last part.

Ida Henderson isn't fooling anyone. Her granddaughter is really her daughter, shipped off for someone else to raise. Marcie's imagination took hold of her. That stuffed, ruffled blouse didn't hide a heart, she told herself. She looked through the church files and discovered Ida had children on record. Marcie had never heard about them. Must have been before her time. Hard to believe Ida had ever been a mother. She figured she needed to change her narration, but no, this is fiction. She could write what she wanted.

Marcie stopped typing and flipped her laptop shut as Pastor Joe approached.

"Did you finish updating the church census?"

"Done."

"Really? Let me see."

"Well it's not quite ready for you to look at it."

"I thought as much. When you finish, I'd like a copy on my desk."

"Sure thing, Captain," Marcie knew that it irritated Pastor when she called him captain but he didn't correct her this time. Shoot, maybe she would have to come up with another term to rile him, she thought.

Updating the parish census was easy work. Boring, tedious, time consuming, but easy. So much more fun to make up stories.

"Marcie, would you come in here?" Pastor Joe called her into his office.

"Now what?" she thought, but dutifully came in.

"I don't think you appreciate the importance of your position as secretary. Not only are you keeper of secrets, you have a significant role to play in preserving and transmitting information."

"If secretaries are so important, then why aren't they remembered in history books? Name one famous secretary."

"Baruch. Jeremiah's secretary. He wrote down Jeremiah's oracles. Paul also had secretaries. You don't think he wrote all those letters by himself, do you?"

"I don't know. Never gave it much thought."

"Back in Biblical times, educated individuals could read, but not necessarily write. Writing letters was a costly endeavor. You had to have ink and quills and paper, none of which were readily available. Most likely Paul dictated his letters to a scribe, or secretary."

"That's Biblical times. Name one in modern times."

"Madeline Albright, Secretary of State. Hilary Clinton."

"That's Secretary of State, not a mere church secretary."

"The title's still secretary. King David had a number of scribes serving him, and a secretary of state. They were indispensable to the operation of the kingdom, just as you are indispensable to the operation of this church."

"If you think that makes me feel better about being a lowly secretary, it doesn't."

"No, nothing will make you feel better about it unless you decide you want to feel better."

"It's just that ..." Marcie wasn't sure what she wanted or what she intended to say. The words just slipped out. "I want my life to mean something. I don't want to waste it, not a minute of it."

"Is that what you think I'm doing?"

"No, not you. You help all those people."

"And you make it possible for me to help those people."

"I just want to make a difference. Me."

"Is that your fear?" Joe looked across the desk at Marcie, tapping his fingers.

"What? What are you talking about?"

"Are you afraid that your life doesn't mean anything? That you don't make a difference? Is that why it's so hard for you to settle on anything, not a major in college, not your work here?" Pastor Joe waited for her to respond. When she didn't, he added. "Look, I don't have time for this. You think about whether you want to continue in your position and let me know. I have work to do." Joe started to read some papers on his desk.

Marcie squirmed in her seat. How did he know this? Her dad must have told him. Nothing she had tried had seemed important enough to dedicate her life to it. Everything interested her at first, until it didn't. She had thought about medicine but found all the science boring and mind-numbing. Then she had considered pre-vet. Animals were more interesting than humans, but again there was all that science, and pre-vet was even more competitive than pre-Med. She didn't know whether she could get into Veterinary school. And if she did, she dreaded the thought of all those years of school. Her dad had suggested pre-law.

"It's a nice general major that would prepare you for a lot of different careers." But the thought of having to study all those laws and having to read all that legalese made her eyes cross. She even considered ministry. At least that seemed meaningful. She would be a doctor of souls rather than a doctor of bodies. But the ministers she knew were too stuffy for her tastes, like Pastor Joe. They had to be too good. That wasn't her. She wanted to do something meaningful, but she wanted to have fun at the same time.

"If only I were good at something creative, like art or music. If only I had stuck with dance classes or piano lessons or had gone out for band in high school. Maybe I could have had a career as an artist," she thought. But she hadn't. Nothing appealed to her. And so she had dropped out. The pressure to decide on a major and stick with it was just too much.

That was when she had decided to try her hand at writing. It didn't take years of schooling. Anyone who knew how to type and had basic computer skills could write a blog. And it was fun. She could write about anything and anyone she wanted. No papers to hand in, no grades to worry about and she could set her own deadline. It was perfect, until it wasn't.

"You still here?" Pastor Joe looked up and saw her.

"Oh, I'm sorry." Marcie got up and returned to her desk. She opened up her laptop and reached for her coffee.

Now where was she, she asked herself as she turned on her computer.

Chapter 7

"Jeremy Long is here to see you." Marcie pushed the intercom button.

"Send him in," Pastor Joe's disembodied voice sounded back at her. Marcie directed Jeremy to the pastor's open door. She heard a loud welcome as Jeremy walked in. She imagined the scene, a strong handshake then a hug. Pastor Joe was a hugger, at least of those he knew and liked. He had yet to hug her. Marcie felt bristles coursing along her spine at the thought. No, she did not want to be hugged by the pastor. He was the boss after all.

She wondered what brought Jeremy to see the pastor. Maybe an extramarital affair to confess? Or maybe it was his wife having the affair. Jeremy just wasn't the affair type.

"Like you would know," her left brain interrupted.

"I just know these things," the right responded.

"Very well then." Marcie knew the Longs had five school-aged children. Maybe he needs help with money, she thought. Must be hard providing for five children and a wife. Rumor has it she was pregnant with their sixth child. As far as she knew, his wife didn't work outside the home. That's it. She's an alcoholic, hiding at home behind his children.

"Don't be ridiculous. They are pillars of the church," the internal dialogue continued.

"Then why is he coming to see the pastor? He has to have some problem."

And then there was that other couple, Dale and Ava. Marcie vaguely remembered Dale's first wife, Joy, from taking classes at the dance studio when she was little. Her dad had thought it was important that she not miss out on any of the little girl necessities of life just because she didn't have a mom around, so he had enrolled her in ballet classes. Dance classes had been fun at first. And who doesn't like a tutu and dressing like a princess for recitals? But what she had really wanted was time to ride her bike and play with her friends. It had taken a while for her to convince her dad that he would not be neglecting his parental duties if she quit dance classes.

She had liked Joy. Joy had made the classes fun. She had continued for a while just because of Joy, but even Joy was not enough to keep her inside on a newly warm spring day.

Marcie had never known Joy's husband or her children, yet she had felt a bond with the children because of their loss of their mother. She knew what it was to not have a mother. But you don't miss what you never had, or so she told herself.

She didn't know about this other woman, Ava. She figured she was okay. And then there was Kathleen, Dale's sister. Now she was a mystery. Rumor had it that she had spent time in prison. Rumor had also had it that she was dating the pastor. What was Pastor Joe doing with a jailbird? Kathleen called every day, sometimes two or three times. Pastor always took her calls. His voice changed when he spoke to her. Marcie may not have been able to hear what was said, but she could hear the change in tone. He smiled more, most of the time when Kathleen called, though sometimes she caught a note of exasperation, or was that just whenever Pastor Joe spoke to her? Some days Kathleen breezed in, walked right past her without acknowledging her existence as she let herself into his office.

"Don't get up. I know the way," she would state as she flounced by, in much too big a hurry to pay attention to a lowly secretary.

She hated her. Pastor Joe deserved her. They deserved each other.

Chapter 8

The Case of the Missing Statue
　　"See you next week, Ms. Blossom," Pastor K said as he escorted her out.
　　"Same time, same place, Pastor," the buxom brunette smiled and playfully tugged at his tie before leaving.
　　"You don't have to pretend for my benefit," I told the pastor after she left.
　　"Pretend what?"
　　"You know. By the way, Mrs. Mandelbaum called while you were 'in conference'. Said she needed to see you immediately. I made an appointment for ten."
　　"I thought I had an appointment with Mr. Fiddlesticks at ten."
　　"Changed it. Moved it to two o'clock, which you can always cancel for a hospital emergency."
　　"Good thinking, Sweetstuff. What would I do without you?"
　　I just smiled. I already knew what the emergency of the week was. Mrs. Moneybags had already confided in me. She always stops to chat with me when she comes to see Pastor K. I think I know more about her than the pastor. We are becoming besties.
　　"The statue of St. Luke, the one I had purchased in memory of my late husband, Dr. Mandelbaum. It's gone missing."
　　"Gone missing? That's terrible. Who could have committed such a crime?"
　　"Who indeed? I'll make sure Pastor K does something about it."
　　And I'm sure she will.
　　"Now you let me know as soon as you find out anything," Mrs. Mandelbaum said as she left Pastor K's office. "I'd hate to have to call in the police."
　　"There's no need for that. I'll give this my highest priority. I'm sure we will get to the bottom of this." Pastor K assured her.
　　"Pastor," I said after she left. "Wasn't that the statue the worship committee decided to move out of the sanctuary?"
　　"The same."
　　"So, what are you going to tell Mrs. Mandelbaum?"

Kathleen approached the group of teen girls sharing something on their phones and giggling.

"What's so interesting?" The girls jumped apart, straightened up and hid their phones.

"Nothing, Ms. Reese." They shifted their feet and avoided her gaze. Kathleen was used to the girls always being on their phones in between classes. This was different.

"Then get to your classes." The girls scampered away. Kathleen knew how to find out what they were up to. She found it amusing how her approach put fear into the girls' hearts. She kind of liked it. She ran a tight ship and they knew it. No monkeying around, no foolishness. She had had enough foolishness at their age and didn't want any more of it.

"Do you know what the girls were giggling about?" she asked Chloe.

"You don't know?"

"No, or why would I be asking you?"

"I just thought, I mean, with you being friends with Pastor Joe and all ..."

Kathleen raised her eyebrow. "What has this to do with Pastor Joe?"

"Not just Pastor Joe, you too."

"Now you've got me even more interested. Tell me."

"I mean, it is Pastor Joe's secretary and all ..." Kathleen waited while Chloe clicked through her phone and showed her a website entitled, *Delicious Secrets*.

"Hmmm," Kathleen read through the post. "Buxom brunette?" she looked at Chloe.

"There's more." Chloe showed Kathleen other posts.

"And you say Joe's secretary is writing this?"

"Has to be. Who else could it be? It's all the girls talk about." Chloe watched as Kathleen continued to flip through the web site. "Do you want me to tell them to stop?"

"Of course not. We can't control what they do on their own time." Chloe shifted from one foot to another while Kathleen perused the phone.

"Don't you have a class to teach?" Kathleen looked over at the young woman.

"Umm, my phone?"

"Oh, yeah, sorry." Kathleen handed the phone back to her. "Now get to work." Kathleen dismissed Chloe.

"Maybe I can have some fun with this," she thought as she watched Chloe walk away.

Unlike the teenage assistants, Chloe wasn't fooled by Kathleen's external demeanor. Kathleen had supported her in her own, inimical way. Throughout her pregnancy last year, then through her daughter's birth and her grandfather's death last fall. She knew Kathleen was someone she could count on, though she didn't want to push her too far. Chloe had struggled to take on the position left by her friend Letty last summer. Kathleen had been patient with her as she learned the ropes of managing a dance studio along with teaching multiple classes. She was so good with Mary, her daughter. Kathleen watched Mary crawl around her office while Chloe taught. She would bounce her on her hip while talking to parents of students.

"You know, you're a natural at this," her brother Dale had once quipped to Kathleen. In response he had received an icy stare.

"Don't be getting any ideas," Kathleen had told him.

"I'm not getting ideas. I'm just saying." Dale was recently remarried after losing his wife to cancer not quite four years earlier. In his current state of honeymoon bliss, he appeared to be playing cupid for his big sister. He, too, was aware of the on-again, off-again, nature of Kathleen's relationship with Pastor Joe.

Chloe had witnessed the exchange between brother and sister and smiled to herself. Only Kathleen's brother Dale could get away with making such suggestions, and maybe her mother, Esther. It definitely was a family affair, the dance studio and the Center for the Arts. Joy had started it, but over time Joy's mother-in-law and sister-in-law had come on board. After her death, Joy had left the building, and all the expenses involved, to Kathleen.

Chloe hadn't been around for this. She had only learned second-hand about how the dance studio had come to be and had ended up in the unlikely hands of Kathleen Reese. Chloe would have thought Kathleen to be the hard-nosed owner of a local drinking establishment, or even a madam of a brothel, before being in charge of a dance studio, and especially one with the tag-line, Dancing for the Lord. She loved the irony of the situation. Perhaps the blog was rubbing off on her, Chloe thought, as she imagined Kathleen in a past life running a bar in a western locale, keeping the cowboys in line and dating the local sheriff.

Chloe had been enjoying the blog, *Delicious Secrets*, as much as her assistants, giggling behind their backs as she read each word. She didn't want the girls to know she read the posts, lest she lose her thin veneer of authority over them. That was what Kathleen was for, she figured, to enforce her position and help her maintain discipline with a group of undisciplined dancers and instructors. And yet dance was all about discipline. You had to work very hard to make it look easy, she reminded herself. She enjoyed her guilty pleasures, scoops of ice cream now and then, and reading *Delicious Secrets* as she made up her own secrets.

Dale was a frequent visitor to the studio as he and his wife, Ava, took turns picking up his children. Since giving up on her Irish step dance classes, Ashley, Dale's oldest daughter, had become a focused student of ballet. Ashley had finally acquired the coveted pointe shoes and appeared ready to follow in her mother's footsteps as a dancer. Chloe had been disappointed to lose her most promising step dancer, but pleased that she hadn't given up dancing completely, something she had been afraid might happen her first year at the studio. Ashley also was a trusted babysitter as she grew into a mature twelve-year-old. Jacob, Dale's son, at ten had refused to continue attending classes. He had tried step dancing for a year but quickly gave it up. He still rode the bus to the studio every day after school, did homework and played until picked up. Grace, a pudgy seven-year-old, was far from her name, yet she enjoyed the classes, favoring tap dance over ballet where her extra pounds were less of a hindrance.

Completing the family was Esther, Kathleen's mother, keeper of the center's accounts and a mother and grandmother to the instructors and students. She could be found keeping late hours with her glasses sliding down her nose. She often waited until every student left the building. Joined by her husband of two years, Peter, they helped Chloe lock up at night.

"You know, you don't have to help me lock-up. I can handle it." And she could, with a little assist from Officer Nash, her boyfriend, when he was off duty, and even some times when he was on duty.

"With a baby in tow?" Esther contradicted her, then would see Officer Nash. "Maybe you can. Humor us."

Chloe did appreciate the help since most nights she had Mary with her, and especially since she no longer had her grandfather at home, waiting for her with a bowl of soup and a sandwich. Her grandfather had left her his house along with a sum of money for its upkeep and her own living expenses. Enough to help her get by.

"Are you sure you don't want us to come home with you? Make sure you get inside safely?" Peter always asked on those nights it was dark by the time she left and Officer Nash was nowhere to be found.

"No," Chloe always insisted, though they followed her home anyway, always watching out for her safety. She would unlock her door, then turn and wave at them.

"Busted," Peter would say as they waved back. They waited until she was safely inside, then drove away.

Yes, it was a family business, and Chloe was part of the family.

Chapter 9

Mr. Fiddlesticks or the Case of the Missing Pastor

"Oh, no, here he comes again," Pastor K said as an older man was seen on the sidewalk approaching the church office. "Tell him I'm not available."

"But your car is in your parking place."

"Tell him I'm in conference."

"Then he'll want to wait for you to be done."

"Then tell him I have an out-of-town meeting and car pooled with someone else. Tell him whatever you have to."

"Okay, Pastor." Mr. Fiddlesticks was newly retired from his job managing the largest grocery store in town. He needed something to fill his time. His wife wouldn't let him stay home and rearrange her life, so he was trying to run the church. Daily he called with suggestions for the pastor as to how to run the church more efficiently.

"But the church isn't a business," I've heard Pastor K tell him repeatedly. It did no good.

"Nonsense. It's God's business and the people's money. You have to be a good steward of the people's money. In the end it's all about money."

Pastor K has taken to avoiding him at all costs. He doesn't take Mr. Fiddlesticks' calls anymore, doesn't return his calls, and so Mr. Fiddlesticks has started showing up at all hours hoping to catch Pastor K in.

"But where is he? His car is here?"

"He had a meeting. At church headquarters."

"How did he get there?"

"One of the other local ministers drove. Do you want to leave a message?"

"No wonder the church is always in the red. How can he run the church when he's never here? You let me into his office and I'll wait for him," Mr. Fiddlesticks insisted.

"But he may go straight home without checking his messages when he gets back."

"I don't care. Let me in."

"I can't do that ..." I started to say but before I could stop him, Mr. Fiddlesticks had opened the office door. Pastor K was nowhere to be found.

"I'll wait," Mr. Fiddlesticks proclaimed.

Now how did Pastor K escape? Was it true about those tunnels rumored to be between church rectories and nunneries (not that Pastor K was Catholic, but protestant ministers are known to have their secrets too)? Did he climb out the window? I didn't see any open windows. Or did he suddenly develop the gift of teleportation? What do you think?

Stay tuned to find out as we continue the adventures of St. Everybody!

SS

"What are you two talking about?" Esther asked Kathleen and Chloe

"We are talking about what everybody is talking about, Mom. A blog. All about people's secrets."

"A secret blog?"

"No, a blog about secrets. *Delicious Secrets*. Here, look." Kathleen handed her phone to Esther.

"That's interesting." Esther went through the posts. "I wonder if she has written anything about me."

"About you? What would she write about you?" Kathleen asked

"I have my secrets."

"You do?"

"Of course I do. Doesn't everybody?" Esther responded.

"Tell us them, Esther," Chloe entered the conversation.

"You don't want to hear my secrets," Kathleen told her mom.

"Oh, you'd be surprised how much I know. Not a lot happens at Cascade Falls without it getting back to me. At least where you were concerned. All those times slipping out of the house when you thought I was asleep. The clothes and jewelry you showed up with and those characters you hung out with. Don't get me started."

"You don't know the half of it," Kathleen insisted.

"And you're right. I'd rather not know."

"But what about you, Esther? What are your secrets?" Chloe asked.

"Yeah, Mom. Tell us."

"Well, I bet you thought I didn't date anyone all those years, raising you, then raising Josh and Scott."

"If you did, you kept it well hidden," Kathleen said.

"That was the idea. I couldn't bring just anybody into your life. And then again, a widow with two kids. How many men wanted to take that on, especially once they met you?" Esther pointed at Kathleen.

"Me? Why I was a darling child."

"You weren't exactly a selling point. Most men, they met you and they ran," Esther said.

"What are you talking about? You never brought anyone home to meet us."

"I had my ways. Remember those church picnics and potlucks during the winter?"

"Yeah, but no one came and sat with us. Or if they did, they didn't stay long," Kathleen said.

"Ever wonder why?" Esther asked.

"Well, I do remember now. I remember that guy with the lazy eye and suspenders. He tried to give me some candy. I told him my mama said not to ever take candy from strangers, then I snapped his suspenders and ran, yelling, 'Stranger, stranger!' You weren't dating him, were you?" Kathleen grinned.

"Not after that. And he didn't have a lazy eye," Esther contradicted Kathleen.

"And then there was that guy with the mustache and pocket watch. I liked his pocket watch."

"So much that you stole it from him."

"Well, he shouldn't have been showing it off so. It was like he was asking to have it stolen." Kathleen laughed as she remembered. "I'm sorry, Mom, if I chased away your beaus."

"If it had been serious, they wouldn't have been so easy to chase off. A real man wouldn't have been scared off so quickly. Like this guy here." Esther pointed at Peter as he joined the group.

"What are you talking about?" Peter asked.

"Mom's telling us about her boyfriends before you," Kathleen told him.

"Oh, that so? Are you keeping something from me?"

"No secrets from you, dear." Esther winked at Kathleen. "But then there was that one young man ..."

"Tell us," Chloe and Kathleen said.

"Yes, tell us," Peter added.

"Not much to tell. It was before your father and I started dating. Seems he was rich, though I didn't know it at the time."

"Oooh, tell more," Kathleen and Chloe teased.

"He had gotten himself into some trouble so his parents had shipped him off to live with his grandparents for a while. Andrew Dean Richardson was his name."

"Not from the Richardson Hardware Store chain?" Peter asked.

"The same."

"How'd you let him get away, Mom?"

"I didn't exactly let him get away. I never had him. We dated for a while in high school. Grandpa didn't approve of him."

"So, Mom, you dated a bad boy?"

"I don't know that I would call him that."

"What would you call it?" Kathleen asked.

"Maybe just someone who had lost his way."

"A lost boy. And you were going to save him."

"Nonsense. Anyway, he went back home to his parents and your dad and I started dating and that's the end of it. I never heard anything about him since." Esther dismissed the idea.

"Maybe you should try looking him up," Kathleen suggested.

"Hey, I am right here, you know," Peter cut in.

"No offense, Peter, but if Mom had a rich boyfriend ..."

"Again, I'm right here," Peter said.

"Don't worry about it, Peter." Esther put her hand on his arm. "I'm perfectly happy as I am, though I do wonder what happened to him."

"See, Mom, we could look him up, see what he is up to."

"No, some secrets are better left to the imagination." Esther tried to end the conversation.

"What does that mean?" Peter asked.

"Nothing, dear." Esther smiled. "Just sweet memories. Andrew had been a bit of a bad boy. It had been fun going out with him, a little danger and excitement. I had thought, maybe I could save him from himself, make him a better person," Esther had mused. "Anyway, it was nothing. Nothing for you to know. My secret," she stated as she took Peter's arm. "Time to go."

"So what kind of secrets are you keeping?" Kathleen asked Chloe after Peter and Esther left.

"What do you mean? There's Mary, but she's no secret."

"Oh, come on. All those years in New York. Dancing on stage. Late night parties. I bet you have some great secrets hidden away."

"My life in New York was surprisingly tame, despite what you think."

"Chloe?" Kathleen reached for Chloe's arm and started to twist it behind her back.

"No, I mean it. There's nothing to tell. I mean, New York was New York. Lots of excitement, Broadway, Central Park, but most of my time was spent just trying to make a living. It wasn't exactly cheap living there."

"You still can't fool me. I bet there's something there, something you aren't telling me. But I'll let you off the hook for now. By the way, what have you told that young man of yours?"

"About what?"

"About Mary, of course."

"He knows about Mary."

"But how much? What about Mary's father?"

"What about him?" Chloe could feel anxiety crawling up her neck.

"I mean, have you told him who he was and that he is still in your life?"

"Mary's life. He's in Mary's life, not my life. And that's no business of yours. I don't talk to him on a regular basis. I haven't seen him since that one time last spring. He hasn't even met Mary yet. That's how he wants it. If it wasn't for Letty, he wouldn't even know about Mary. Letty's the one who sees him and tells him about Mary."

"But, is that how you want it?"

"As far as I'm concerned, I don't care if I ever see him again. I only keep any contact with him for Mary's sake."

"If you say so. And what are you going to tell Mary about her father when she gets older?"

"The truth. That her father is a dancer on Broadway. You know, you do like to stir up trouble, don't you? What business do you have bringing all this up? No wonder your mom never had any boyfriends when you were around."

"I couldn't let my mom go out with those losers."

"So, you knew all along what you were doing?"

"It wasn't hard to figure out, all those men at church. But I think it's best my mom doesn't know, right?" Kathleen gave Chloe a conspiratorial glance.

"I'll keep your secret, if you keep mine," Chloe said.

"Which one?"

"All of them. Even the ones I don't know yet."

Kathleen laughed. "Sure, I guess I can do that."

After Kathleen left, Chloe picked up Mary, hugged her and whispered, "I'll never have any secrets from you."

Chapter 10

Delicious Secrets - Mr. & Mrs. Two-timers

The Two-timers were speaking with Pastor K again. They merit this name, not because they are cheating on each other, but because this is the second marriage for both. After they both had been divorced from their first spouses, Miss Icantbealone quickly latched onto to Mr. Gottohavesomeone. They were married posthaste, even as the ink was drying on their divorce decrees. Is it any wonder they were back to see the pastor as soon as the honeymoon was over?

"What brings you here?" I asked Mrs. Two-timers while her husband excused himself to use the facilities. "Certainly there were no problems with the wedding night, you both being married before."

"Oh, no. It's not that at all. Mr. Two-timers is great. It's just..." Mrs. Two-timers looked about to make sure no one could hear her then whispered, "It's those children. You have no idea what it's like marrying into a ready-made family. They hate me." Mrs. Two-timers started to sob as Mr. Two-timers returned to the room.

"Eve, are you starting again?" Mr. Two-timers frowned. "We haven't even gotten in to see the pastor yet and here you are crying."

I gave Mrs. Two-timers a tissue and conciliatory nod. "It must be hard."

"You don't know the half of it. That Rowena is evil. I'm sure she's possessed. Any day now her head will start to spin."

"Don't talk nonsense," Mr. Two-timers said.

"Really," I said, ignoring Mr. Two-timers' remark.

"Yes, really." Mrs. Two-timers leaned in closer. "The other day I found her in my bedroom going through my drawers. She stuffed something in her pocket when I walked in then accused me of spying on her."

"Indeed. What a terrible thing to say."

"Later," Mrs. Two-timers continued, "I looked in her room and found a small doll made out of one of my handkerchiefs with pins in it."

"How dreadful," I said.

"You know, I have secrets too," Ashley said to no one in particular on
the way home from the dance studio.

"What are you talking about?" Dale looked over at his oldest
daughter. In the back of the car, Jacob was playing video games and
Grace was gazing off into space.

"All everybody at the dance studio talks about is this blog about
secrets. I have secrets too."

"Who's everybody?"

"Janene, Isabel, Darcy, Hannah," Ashley listed the names of the
teen instructors.

"Oh, that everybody."

"They think I'm not old enough to understand, to be included in
their clique."

Why hadn't he let Ava pick the kids up when she had offered,
Dale thought. Then she could have addressed this drama. She was
much better at it than he was.

"Well, you are younger than them." Ashley shot him a glance
intended to make the staunchest of hearts shrivel into a lump of Jello.
Fortunately, he had years of dealing with such looks from growing up
with Kathleen. "What do the other girls in your class think?" he
boldly ventured on.

"Dad, they're just kids."

"Aren't they the same age as you?"

"Yeah, but they're not like me."

"Oh," Dale wondered what to say next. Fortunately, Ashley filled
in the silence.

"I've got secrets, too, just like Janene and them. But nobody is interested in what I have to say."

"I'm interested. You can tell me."

"That's because you're my dad. You're the last person I would tell my secrets."

"Oh," Dale was relieved to be off the hook. "Would you tell Ava?"

"My stepmother? Ewww. No way, Dad. You just don't understand. Nobody understands."

Ashley jumped out of the car, stomped off into the house and upstairs to her room the minute he pulled into the driveway, running past Ava as she went through the door.

Dale grabbed Grace's backpack from where she had left it in the back seat and handed it to her.

"Grace, here. Didn't you forget something?" Grace just looked at the backpack and took it from him.

Lost in her own world, Dale thought as he followed after his youngest. Jacob dragged his backpack on the ground, his attention still riveted on his game.

"What was that all about?" Ava asked him as she gave him a welcoming kiss.

"At least someone is happy to see me," he told her.

"Of course I'm happy to see." Ava gave him a longer kiss.

"Ewww, do you two always have to do that?" Ashley appeared at the top of the stairs.

"No," Dale caught his breath. "We do it to annoy you."

"Well, you're succeeding. I'll be up in my room, if anyone cares. When is supper?"

"Good question." Dale looked at Ava. "Is supper ready?"

"Depends on how much help I get. About twenty minutes." This was Dale's cue to follow her into the kitchen.

"So, what was that all about?" Ava asked again.

"You mean this?" Dale wrapped his arms around her and started to kiss her again.

"No," Ava pushed him away with a laugh. "You know what I mean."

"Right. Something about some blog about secrets."

"*Delicious Secrets*. All the teachers are talking about it."

"So, it's real."

"It sure is, and your sister is a recurring star."

"What are you talking about?"

"It's all about this fictional church, the Church of St. Everybody with Pastor Knowitall in some 'fictional' town called Cascades. Everybody knows it's about St. Luke's."

"How do they know that?"

"Just read it," Ava said, then added, "After dinner. I need your full attention now." She gave him a kiss and handed him dishes. "Set the table."

Lucky followed Ashley upstairs and jumped up on the bed with her.

"You're the only one who understands." Ashley cradled the mutt in her arms. Brindle color with a lab's body and bull dog face, Lucky had become part of the family during her mother's illness. He continued to be a support and confidant. Ashley pulled her homework from her backpack and turned on her music.

Grace came into the bedroom they shared and sat down on her bed. Ashley glared at her, then ignored her. Grace picked up two of her dolls and proceeded to have them engage in a conversation.

"I'm trying to do my homework," Ashley said over the music.

"It's my room too," Grace said, then threw a stuffed monkey at her sister. In the past this would have provoked a friendly war with stuffed animals flying about the room. Not today.

"Quit it, brat." Ashley tossed the monkey aside.

Grace went to the top of the stairs and yelled down, "Daddy, Ashley's being mean to me."

Dale looked at Ava and sighed before going to the bottom of the stairs. "Why don't you play downstairs?"

"It's my room, too."

"I know." Dale looked up at his youngest. She was the same age as Ashley had been when her mom's cancer had recurred. That was where the resemblance ended. Grace was nothing like her sister. No one was like Ashley. "Come on down and you can help set the table."

"Okay," Grace agreed. She actually liked helping out around the house. So unlike her sister.

"Hmmm," Dale said as he sat in bed and read the last post on the blog. "Interesting."

"Is that all you have to say."

"Never thought of Kathleen as a buxom brunette."

"You do agree it's St. Luke's, don't you?"

"I don't know. It could be any liberal, small-town church."

"With a widowed pastor with two college-aged daughters?"

"Okay. It does sound like St. Luke's. So what? What does that have to do with us?"

"What about the post about the newlyweds?"

"You think that's us?" Dale asked.

"You tell me." Ava took Dale's tablet out of his hands. "What does this have to do with Ashley? What did she say?"

"She feels left out. Seems all the older girls at the studio are talking about the blog but they are not talking to her."

"Ashley is mature for her age. Emotionally she fits in with the older group, but they won't accept her. She doesn't really fit with the kids her age. That's a hard place to be, especially at her age when peers are so important."

"Maybe you can talk to her."

"I don't know. I'm still the dreaded stepmom." Ava and Ashley had come to an understanding last year before Ava would agree to marry Dale, but that didn't mean they were best friends now.

"Then who?"

"Maybe Chloe?" Chloe had become friends with Ashley while driving her to step dance classes last year. Now Ashley was a regular guest at Chloe's home, helping with Mary. "Or Kathleen." Kathleen had helped Ashley during the months of her mom's illness and death. "Or maybe we just stay available and wait for an opportunity to be supportive if it presents itself."

"With Ashley, that could be a long wait."

"I know," Ava agreed. "I know," she repeated then handed Dale's tablet back to him. "Do you think we are like that couple? The one on the blog."

"The Two-timers? Us? Of course not. It's all made up. I can't believe anyone reads this crap. I can't believe you read it." Dale was surprised at the anger creeping into his voice. He was usually the calm, level-headed one. Too much for one night.

"I mean, maybe we did get married too soon. Maybe we should have waited longer. Do you think I can't stand to live alone?"

"Don't talk nonsense. We waited four years. Four years after Joy's death."

"Not quite four years."

"Close enough. And remember, it was over a year and a half before we even went out on a date. I had a hard time convincing you at that."

"I guess."

"Don't guess. I know. Now go to sleep." Dale turned off the light and wrapped his arms around Ava as she fell asleep. Then he pulled his arm out from under her still body and turned over, trying to sleep.

Chapter 11

"Bernie Rogers is back in town." Gwen was taking in the last rays of sun sliding down the horizon behind the band shell.

Marcie pushed back her floppy hat and looked at Gwen. "Really?" she feigned indifference.

"Yes, I saw him at the café yesterday. Said he was in town for the summer, visiting his grandparents."

"Hmmm," Marcie leaned further back in the lawn chair as she gazed across the lawn to where her young charges were playing while a band played in the band shell. Not her type of music, but it was better than staying cooped up in her neighbor's home all night. This way the kids would be tired when she got them home. She could put them to bed then stream a movie till their parents returned. Marcie kicked off her sandals and let her feet luxuriate in the grass. She loved the freedom of wearing sandals. Her feet could breathe and so could she. She collected multiple pairs in her closet and waited all winter for the first opportunity to put them on.

The band was playing oldies. Her dad should be here, she thought. She remembered coming to the band shell with him when she was small. Children rolled down the slope of the hill. Others danced in front of the band shell. Her lips curled playfully as a young couple danced. They looked all of six. About her age when she had first met Bernie.

She remembered another couple of kids, playing on the hill, dancing to the music, chasing after each other, hanging over the edge of the dock and looking for fish. Seemed not that long ago. They would hold hands and run in circles until they both fell down in the grass and watched the stars swirl above. And then there were the fireworks, Memorial Day weekend, Fourth of July and Labor Day weekend. He had lived a few houses down from her house. She would walk to the park with her dad and meet him there.

"Daddy ..."

"Go on," her dad would respond before she even got the words out. He knew, much as she loved him, he was no substitute for someone her own age.

And so, Bernie and she had played all summer, until he had moved away, not saying goodbye, not telling her where he was going. He had just gone. She had seen the car being packed and ran outside to watch it pull away.

That had been the last she had seen of Bernie until high school. He had returned as unexpectedly as he had left, moving in with his grandparents. She didn't know what had happened to his parents. Bernie had not wanted to talk about it. They had picked up where they had left off. Riding bikes, walking to school together, going to the park, hanging out.

"Hey," a young man in a cowboy hat flopped down in the grass next to her. A large hound dog flopped next to him. Marcie raised the brim of her floppy hat and stared.

"Bernie?"

"None other." He said. "And this here is Blade."

She removed her hat and knocked his hat off with it. "How could you come back and not call me?"

"I knew you would be here. I wanted to surprise you."

"No surprise. Gwen just told me she saw you in the coffee shop." Gwen leaned forward in her chair and smiled at him.

"Maybe it's time I left," Gwen said.

"No way, stay here." Marcie placed her hand on Gwen's wrist to keep her from getting up.

"Sure, stay. There's no reason for you to leave. We're just old friends getting together." Bernie reached for his hat and placed it firmly on his head.

"And what is the deal with that hat?" Marcie asked.

"You know I love playing guitar."

"So ..."

"So, I'm in a country band."

"In Michigan?"

"No, Tennessee, Nashville, Grand Ole Opry and all that."

"I know about the Opry." Marcie looked to the right, avoiding his gaze as she looked for her young charges. "So, how did you end up there?"

"Long story. You got time?"

"Actually, no, I don't. Not right now. I'm babysitting."

"I don't see any babies."

"Over there, on the swings. Mark and Audrey. My neighbor's kids."

"Remember when we were that age, playing on the swings?" Bernie's voice waxed sentimental. He had a way of speaking that made Marcie forget herself.

"How could I forget? I never went anywhere but here, dull old Cascade Falls."

"Last I heard you had gone away to college."

"Well, that didn't last too long. Now I'm back here. Not like you. Where did you go?" Marcie fought the lure of his voice.

"Oh, you know. The usual. Where else would a young man with a broken heart go?"

"You left me, remember?"

"That's not exactly how I remember it."

"Then you remember it wrong." Marcie felt a flush of anger grasp her around her ribs. How dare he, she thought. She resisted the urge to knock off more than his hat.

"Anyway," Bernie shifted uncomfortably on the ground. "Eventually I ended up in Nashville. I got a job as a dishwasher in a bar and graduated to guitar player in a band. What about you?"

"Not much to tell."

"She's working at ..." Marcie stomped on Gwen's foot to shut her up. There was no way she wanted to tell him she was a lowly church secretary, him with his cowboy boots and hat.

"Hey," Gwen rubbed her foot and glared at Marcie who glared back. "It really is time for me to go now." Gwen stood up and folded her chair.

"Time for me to go too." Marcie stood up and called, "Mark, Audrey."

"Wait," Bernie jumped to his feet, took Marcie by the hand and placed his other hand on her hip, swaying to the music. "Remember how we used to dance?"

How could she forget? Marcie felt it throughout her body, his touch, his breath on her neck.

"I've got to go," she insisted as she pulled away.

"Get coffee with me?" He refused to let go of her hand.

"I don't know." She tried to pull her hand free.

"It's just coffee, for old time's sake. I won't let you go until you say yes."

"Okay," Marcie agreed then tried again to free her hand.

"When? How about tomorrow?"

"I have to work," Marcie fought to come up with an excuse, any excuse, but none were forthcoming.

"After work."

"Okay. Three-thirty at the Coffee Company."

"I'll be there," he said as he let go of her hand. Marcie watched as Bernie and Blade sauntered off down the hill. Gwen walked to the swings with her.

"What was that all about?" Gwen asked once Bernie was out of earshot.

"I don't want him to know I work for the church."

"What's wrong with that?"

"Everything. It's not what I always dreamed of. And now he's living the dream, playing in a band. Promise me you won't tell him." Marcie looked Gwen full in the face, waiting for her response.

"I promise, but I don't see what the big deal is."

You would if you were me, Marcie thought. But you're not. There was too much history. Bernie was the one, always in trouble at school, the one voted the least likely to succeed if they had had a vote on it. She was the one who had known what she was going to do, at least back then. The first thing she had been going to do was get out of Cascade Falls. The second was to forget him. It had taken some time. She thought she was over him. So what was he doing back in her life? Why had she agreed to coffee?

"It's only coffee," her right brain told her.

"You know it's never just coffee where Bernie is concerned," her left brain responded.

"Hush," she told her brain, but it refused to shut down. If only she could turn off her brain like she turned off her laptop.

Marcie and Gwen called it a day.

"Do we have to go?" Mark whined.

"It's still light out," Audrey countered. "Mom lets us play outside until the streetlights are on."

"The streetlights will be on by the time we get home." Marcie remembered the same rules when she had been their age, only it had been her dad, not a mom, setting the rules. "If you behave, we'll have ice cream when you get home."

Mark and Audrey unglued themselves from the swings and came willingly.

"Call me," Gwen said as they parted. "Let me know how coffee goes."

Marcie dismissed Gwen's remark. She wished it was that easy to dismiss Bernie.

Chapter 12

What's in a Name?

You may ask – why is the church called St. Everybody? Well, the church is one of those slightly new-age, non-denominational churches that are open to everybody and doesn't want to offend anyone. Hence the name. Not to be confused with the Church of What's Happening Now.

In the Church of St. Everybody, there are to be no specific saints, lest you offend someone. However, the previous Pastor had allowed the statue of St. Luke because Mrs. Mandelbaum was their biggest donor. The trick was to find a way to placate both sides. Pastor K was still learning this balancing act.

And then there was managing the two biggest donors, Mrs. Mandelbaum and Mrs. Henderson. But more on that later.

"Crap," Marcie muttered under her breath and stopped typing. You had to watch your language when you worked for a church. She had broken a fingernail. Immediately the words of the song from her childhood went through her head – "Found a peanut, found a peanut …"

The verses that played out in her mind were the ones where she broke her fingernail, said a naughty word and was banished from heaven to hell. That was most likely where she was headed, she figured. Bernie had taught it to her when they were kids. The song went on and on and on until you ended where you started from and began again. He had delighted in torturing her with the song.

What was she to do about the nail? Could she squeeze in a manicure before she met Bernie? Most likely not. There just wasn't enough time even if she could get an appointment. Maybe if she got out of work early … Pastor Joe had become wise to her trick. No, better that she stay until three o'clock like she was supposed to. What did it matter if her nails were less than perfect? It was only Bernie, after all, only Bernie … her mind trailed off down the rabbit hole that was

Bernie Rogers. She grabbed ahold of it before it could get too far away and lost forever.

"Something wrong?" She jumped at the sound of Pastor Joe's voice.

"No, nothing."

"You sure?" Joe looked intently at her face. She didn't like the attention.

"Yes, I'm fine."

"Well, if you are done with the bulletin, you can leave early today if you want." Marcie didn't know why he offered this to her. It was not like him. Usually he was practically tying her to her chair to ensure she put in her required hours. Maybe he was feeling generous?

"No, I'm fine. I'll stay. Someone has to answer the phone after all."

"Okay. I'm going home. If anyone needs me, you know how to reach me."

Marcie saw Pastor Joe look back over his shoulder and shake his head as she nervously ran a file over her nails. She waved her hand at him to send him on his way, then went back to her nails.

There, not good as new, but passable, Marcie thought as she repaired her nail. She was in no hurry to leave. If anything, she was hoping for an emergency, any excuse to stay longer and miss her coffee date.

She looked at her nails and wondered. What was it about painted nails that appealed to her? She had never really gotten into a lot of "girlie" things growing up but for some reason she liked the look of nails, newly polished, sparkling. She liked trying new colors, sometimes painting each nail a different color.

Her aunt had introduced her to the smell of newly lacquered nails as a favor to her dad. He had been told it was a way to keep her from biting her nails, and it was. How could anyone bite a nail that was so beautiful? She had to find another way to express her nervous agitation. But it hadn't worked. She stopped biting her nails, at least as long as they were newly polished. Instead she found herself picking at the polish as it showed signs of peeling. And then they were back inside her mouth as she nervously bit a hangnail.

She had to have something to do with her fingers when she wasn't biting them, something to occupy her hands. Perhaps that was why she liked writing – something to keep her hands busy and out of trouble. She didn't have long nails. That interfered too much with everything she wanted to do each day, including typing and plucking a few chords on a guitar. But nicely painted nails never got in the way.

Her aunt had taken her for her first real manicure when she had been sixteen. That had been before her junior prom. Aunt Jean had taken her dress and shoe shopping, then took her to get her hair done, all the roles a mother would have fulfilled. Marcie had not known anything about getting dressed up, much less how to fix her hair. She usually wore it pulled up into a pony tail. She had felt awkward and gawky, coming down the stairs in a long dress and heels, her hair piled on top of her head with stray curls framing her face, nails sparkling. Bernie had looked equally awkward in his suit and tie as he placed a flower on her wrist.

They had agreed to attend together.

"Since we both don't have dates, why not?" he had suggested and she had agreed. She had been chatting with friends when he had interrupted and drawn her from her safety zone and out onto the dance floor for a slow dance.

"Grandma's been giving me lessons," he had commented as he glided about the floor.

"Looks like your grandma should have given me some lessons too," Marcie said as she stepped on his foot, almost tripping.

"Just relax, let me lead," he had told her as he put his hand around her waist and guided her.

"I'm not good at that."

"At what, relaxing or letting someone else lead?"

"Both, I guess."

"Why do you have to be so difficult?" Marcie had felt tears wanting to pop up, from where, she didn't know. They had been below the surface and now threatened to burst forth. She didn't want to be difficult, didn't think she was being difficult. She was just being herself. Why was that so difficult? She would have been better off attending the prom alone than having to put up with this.

"You're the one who is difficult," she had started to say, but it had been hard to get the words out as Bernie had covered her mouth with his mouth. She allowed herself to be kissed, then pulled back. The flicker of light coming off of the overhead globe revealed the outline of his face, a face she had thought to be so familiar, but now it was different. She saw him but with different eyes. Everything had changed in that moment. There he was kissing her, right on the lips, right on the dance floor, right where everyone could see him, in front of everybody else, not that anyone was paying attention to the drama unfolding unbeknownst to them, for each was involved in their own drama. He had kissed her and there was no going back.

Perhaps that's why she liked her nails polished, manicured in a salon. They reminded her of that night. And then he was gone. Like Cinderella, or Cinderfella, slipping off in the night, leaving her behind, only it wasn't that night that he had disappeared out of her life, but the next morning, and he didn't leave a slipper behind as a clue to find him. He was gone again from her life, just as he had gone when she was a girl, after the summer of her seventh year. Again she was left alone and confused.

Why had she agreed to meet him for coffee? She glanced inside the window of the coffeehouse, hoping that maybe he wouldn't show up. But no, there he was, standing, chatting with some other friends from high school. He hadn't seen her look in. She could still slip away unnoticed, she told herself.

She locked her bike and prepared to walk in, fluffing her helmet hair, wondering if she was too sweaty from the ride over. Why hadn't she thought of that before this? She didn't want to meet him like this, red-faced and over-heated from riding her bike, and with a less than perfect nail. But it was only Bernie. She entered the coffee shop.

Bernie smiled, shook hands with the guys he had been talking to, and made his way to her. "What can I get you?" he asked.

"That's okay, I'll get it myself." She walked over to the counter and ordered her usual latte flavored with a hint of chocolate, fussed with the lid before sitting down with Bernie.

"So, where have you been all this time? Where did you go?" she started.

"I was hoping we wouldn't have to talk about that. Can't we talk about the good times, riding our bikes through the park, through the cemetery, along the trails, out to the lake."

"How can you just disappear out of my life, then show up like nothing had happened?"

Bernie grinned at her. "Remember junior prom? You looked gorgeous."

"Is that how it's going to be? No explanation, just picking up where we left off? If that's the case, then I'm out of here." Marcie stood up and prepared to leave. Bernie reached over and placed his hand on her wrist.

"You deserve an explanation, just not here." He looked around the room at the small group of friends he had just left. Her gaze followed his and she realized this was less than ideal for a full confession.

"Let's get out of here." Bernie stood up, picked up his coffee and both headed out the door.

"Where should we meet?" Marcie stopped in front of her bike.

"Our place. I'll load your bike in the back of my truck." Marcie climbed up into the truck next to Blade who slid over into the middle. Bernie easily lifted her bike into the truck bed. "Our place" had been their spot when they were kids and again when they had met up in high school. It was a spot by the pond in the park, semi-secluded by trees and brush. They had sat there, climbed out on a limb that had fallen into the pond and dangled their feet in the water, chased after frogs and tadpoles and thrown rocks across the pond.

"Look at you," Marcie commented as they drove.

"What about me?"

"Here I am, getting around all summer on a bike, having to borrow my dad's car, and here you've got a truck."

"Not much of one, but it gets me where I need to go."

"I mean, who'd have thought when we were in high school, that you would be the success, while I was floundering, stuck in Cascade Falls."

"Cascade Falls is not such a bad place to be, and I wouldn't call what I'm doing a success."

"But you have a career, real goals, while I have nothing."

Bernie pulled into a parking place. Marcie jumped out of the truck and headed for the spot without checking whether he was behind her or not. She wanted to be the one to get there first. That gave her the advantage, she told herself, though why she wanted it or what she would do with it, she didn't know. She kicked off her sandals and dangled her feet in the water.

"Lots of good memories here." Bernie took his place next to her on the limb. Blade lapped up water, then settled down next to the tree trunk.

"So, talk." Marcie wasn't giving him a chance to divert her. Bernie took his time. The minutes dragged by as Marcie waited to hear ... what, she wasn't sure, but some kind of explanation.

"You never really knew my parents, did you?"

"No, you always came over to my house. I never came to your house. I don't know why that was, now that I think of it. It was just understood. It was what we did, I guess."

"Yeah, that was how it was. It was understood. I wasn't allowed to have kids over. But I knew your dad. How is he? I always liked him." Bernie picked up a stone and rubbed the texture between his fingers.

Marcie looked at Bernie, refusing to allow him to change the subject. "What happened? Why did you leave after junior prom the way you did?"

"That was a great night. I've thought about it many times since then."

Marcie continued to look at him as he stared down into the murky water below.

"Well, after that night, after I took you home, there was a problem. My mom, she was in the hospital. My dad called my grandparents, said I needed to come home right away. Said Mom was dying. I didn't believe him. This wasn't the first time Mom had ended up in the hospital. Dad couldn't handle it. He needed me to take care of my brothers so I had to go back. Said that if I didn't take care of them, protective services would put them in foster care."

"Couldn't they have come to live with your grandparents?"

"Then who would have taken care of my mom? No, Dad wanted me back not just to take care of my brothers, but to help clean up after mom. That's the way it had always been. Grandpa loaded my stuff into the car and drove me back that morning. I wanted to go see you, wanted to call, but what would I have said?"

"You could have said you had a family emergency. I would have understood that. What I don't understand is you just leaving the way you did."

"No, I guess you didn't, couldn't. I didn't want to bring you into it, didn't want you or anyone to know. It was the family secret."

"What was?"

"My mom's drinking. She's been in and out of rehab most of my life. The last time though, we thought it had worked. She was clean

and sober for over six months. That had been before I came back to
live with Grandma and Grandpa. We thought she had made it so it was
okay for me to come back here. I had loved it when we lived here. I
had always wanted to come back. And so I had for a while."

"And why did you leave when you were little?"

"Dad had a 'great' job opportunity. He was always getting these
'great' opportunities that had to be acted on right away. I had wanted
to stay with Grandma and Grandpa even then, but he wouldn't let me.
Said he needed me to help Mom around the house when he was away
working."

"But you were only seven."

"Yeah, well, I was an old seven."

"Oh," Marcie's feet played with the water while her mind tried
to take it all in. "I'm sorry."

"She didn't die, not that time, not the next time, though
sometimes I wish she had."

"Don't say that. You don't mean that, do you? Could you?"

"What do you know about life with my mother? You had the
perfect family."

"What are you talking about? I didn't even have a mother."

"And I envied you for that. Having a mother isn't always what
it's cracked up to be. You don't know what life was like, is like, with
my mother. And your dad, he was the best."

"But why didn't you write?"

"And tell you what? That my mom was an alcoholic, my dad had
pretty much abandoned us and I had to raise my brothers and take care
of the family dog? I didn't want your pity."

"You thought I would have pitied you?"

"I don't know what I thought. I wasn't thinking too clearly back
then." Bernie stood up to skip the stone across the pond.

"What happened after that?"

"Pretty much the same story. Mom went into rehab, came home,
was sober for a few days, maybe a few weeks, but she always relapsed.
I never believed her after that. I stuck around long enough for Jake
and Bobby to graduate from high school, then I was out of there. Last
I knew, Mom and Dad were still at it, still repeating the cycle."

"Bernie, I never knew. I'm so sorry."

"Yeah, well, it's good material for song writing. My mom's a
drunk, my dad abandoned us and I lost my dog and my truck."

"Not funny."

"I thought it was." They sat in silence for a while. Bernie stood up to pick up more stones and send them skipping over the water.

"I still can't believe I never noticed anything, not when I was six, nor when I was sixteen," Marcie said.

"When I was six, that was back when my mom still cared enough to maintain a façade of respectability. She made sure our clothes were clean, our faces washed and our stomachs fed before sending us out the door. That changed by the time I was ten. Then I was the one cleaning our clothes, washing faces, feeding stomachs. It also got to be too much for her to go outside when she smoked. No matter how often I washed the clothes, an odor lingered. Kids are cruel. The kindest didn't say anything but they also didn't want to sit next to us because of the smell. Others loudly held their noses and proclaimed, pee-yew!" Bernie held his nose to illustrate.

"Kids can be cruel. I remember being taunted at times because I didn't have a mother. As if it were something I could do anything about. Even when they were silent, I still felt different from other girls, not in a good way. But you didn't care. You never said anything about my mom."

"I'd have hit anyone who said anything to you." Bernie sat back down next to her.

"I know you would have."

"You never said anything about my mom either."

"How could I? I didn't know."

"We were just two misfits." Blade moved closer to Bernie, who reached over and scratched his neck.

"I dealt with it by striving to succeed. I excelled at everything I undertook. And I undertook a lot," Marcie said.

"I remember. You were in every club in high school."

"And if there wasn't one, I started it."

"I dealt with it by rebelling, getting into trouble. Still, you remained my friend." Bernie continued to scratch Blade's neck until he moved back under the tree.

"It wasn't always easy. You didn't make it easy, you and that chip on your shoulder."

"I remember how one teacher took pity on me. I don't know how she knew about what was going on in my home, but one day she took me aside and told me, 'If you soak your clothes in vinegar before you wash them, it will take the smell out.' I tried it and it worked. Fortunately, Dad controlled the money so we had adequate funds for food and cleaning supplies. Dad gave me money for groceries since he couldn't trust Mom. Some days Mom begged me for money. She promised she wasn't going to buy any alcohol, always had a good story to tell to convince me, but I knew better."

"And look at you now."

"Yes, look at me. Look at both of us. All grown up." Bernie stood up again and stretched. Marcie watched but gave him his space.

"So, what's next?" Marcie asked when Bernie sat back down. "How is it you are able to spend the summer with your grandparents?"

"Not the whole summer. Just a month or two break before I have to go back. We've got some gigs scheduled in August, might even be going on tour."

"That's good and bad."

"What do you mean?"

"It's good, you're in a band, you might go on tour, that's good. It's bad, you are only going to be around for a month."

"Or two. We can make the most of it."

"Can we? Only to have you running off again and me never hearing from you?"

"I won't do that this time, Marcie. I promise."

"Can you really promise that? Can I trust you? No more secrets, no more sneaking off and not telling me where you are going or why. Can you promise me that?"

"What if I can't promise that?"

"Then it's best you leave now."

"What if I promise you I will do the best I can? Is that enough?"

Marcie turned away from him, trying to think clearly, rationally, but she couldn't. She never could where Bernie was concerned, at least after that prom night.

"Is that enough?" Bernie asked again.

"I guess it will have to be," Marcie said as he slipped closer to her and kissed her in broad daylight, in the park, but no one was watching except a few squirrels and Blade and even they didn't care. No one cared but her.

Chapter 13

The Case of the Dueling Bank Accounts

There are two large sources of contributions to the Church of St. Everybody, Mrs. Mandelbaum, or Moneybags, and Mrs. Henderson, or Honeybucks. Both considered themselves indispensable to the church, both felt they spoke for the majority of the church congregation and both disliked the other.

One of my responsibilities as church secretary is to schedule appointments in a way to ensure these two do not ever cross paths. This is easier said than done because both women have a tendency to show up unannounced, each confident that Pastor K has nothing better to do than talk to them and that what was uppermost in their minds was of the utmost importance.

This has resulted in a Code Green – Green indicating money.

Pastor K was meeting with Mrs. Moneybags when Mrs. Honeybucks appeared with her dog draped over her shoulder, walking up the sidewalk. I texted Pastor K – Code Green.

Pastor K was annoyed to be interrupted until he saw the message. What to do? He and I had planned for such an occasion. Now was the time to put our plan to the test.

I was to waylay Mrs. Honeybucks in the entryway of the building with small talk while he took Mrs. Moneybags out the side door.

"Wouldn't you like to see where we placed your statue?" Pastor K stood up.

"I saw it last week when it was first placed."

"Oh, but that had been in the morning light. You must see it in the afternoon light. It makes all the difference."

Pastor K led Mrs. Moneybags out the side door and on her way to the grounds. He texted me, "go", to signal that it was okay to bring Mrs. Honeybucks inside.

"Pastor K had to step out for a minute. He'll be back shortly. Why don't you wait in his office?" I escorted her in then went to the window where I saw Pastor K walking with Mrs. Moneybags from the statue to the parking lot. Success. In a few minutes she would be on

her way and Pastor K would be in his office meeting with Mrs. Honeybucks.

Just as Pastor K entered the church office, Mrs. Honeybucks came out of his office.

"I'm afraid Pookie needs to tinkle," she said. "We'll only be a minute."

"Take all the time you need, Mrs. Henderson. I always have time for you," Pastor K said, just as Mrs. Mandelbaum walked in.

"I believe I left my purse in your office ..." She stopped and glared at Mrs. Henderson.

"Ida."

"Harriet."

They said each other's names at the same time, sneering down their noses. I grabbed Mrs. Mandelbaum's purse out of Pastor K's office.

"Why, here's your purse, Mrs. Mandelbaum. So good that you remembered before you got home. Mrs. Henderson, why don't you let me take Pookie outside?"

"Are you sure she'll go with you. She's very particular."

"I'm good with dogs." Pookie bit me as I removed her from her mistress' shoulder. "Here, I'll walk you out," I told Mrs. Mandelbaum, leaving the irascible Mrs. Henderson in the pastor's care.

"The nerve of some people, showing up unannounced," I told Mrs. Moneybags as soon as we were out of earshot.

"Some people can be so demanding," Pastor K told Mrs. Honeybucks as he escorted her into his office. Both of the women commiserated with each of us about the other. Disaster diverted and Code Green was over till another day.

Such is the balancing act required to run a church community. Until the next time,

SS

"What is it everybody keeps talking about?" Erick asked. Erick was Kathleen's grandfather. He had been living with his daughter, Esther, since his wife died, and continued to live in her home along with his new stepson, Peter, and his granddaughter, Kathleen.

Kathleen looked around the table. Ever since her son, Scott, went off to college, at times she felt like she was living in a geriatric ward.

Today was one of those days as she went into the kitchen for coffee and saw her mom, stepdad Peter and Gramps, eating oatmeal. She was grateful that Scott was home for the summer but he was nowhere to be found at that moment.

"It's a blog about secrets, Dad," Esther told him.

Kathleen reached for her phone and pulled up the website. "Here, Gramps." She handed him the phone and helped him maneuver through the blog.

"What's this Church of St. Everybody? Sounds to me like the Church of What's Happening Now. Remember the Flip Wilson Show and Geraldine?" Esther and Peter joined him in laughing.

"Guess that was before my time," Kathleen said, almost smelling a hint of Bengay and bedpans. "So, what about you, Gramps? What are your secrets?"

"You wouldn't want to know."

"Of course I do. Tell us," Kathleen insisted.

"Tell them what?" Scott came into the kitchen in search of coffee.

"Look who finally got up," Esther said as she got up to get Scott some coffee.

"Gramps was about to tell us his secrets," Kathleen said.

"Oh, like that blog," Scott said.

"You know about it too?" Kathleen asked.

"Sure, all my friends are talking about it. What secrets, Gramps?"

"Well, there was this nurse back during the war ..."

"World War II?" Scott asked.

"No, I had been too young for that one. The Korean War. Cutest bob haircut, framed her face perfectly. Button nose." Erick chuckled at the memory.

"Dad," Esther interrupted his memories.

"That was before your mother," he explained.

"That's enough, Dad," Esther told him.

"Ah, I've secrets enough for a life-time. Good ones that I'll keep to my grave."

"You'll share them with me, Gramps, won't you?" Scott asked.

"Maybe some time when your grandmother isn't around," Erick assured Scott.

"What about you, Peter? Do you have any secrets?" Kathleen asked. Esther looked over at her spouse. With only two years of marriage, they were still newlyweds.

"My life is an open book where you are concerned, dear." Peter leaned over and kissed Esther, then winked at Scott.

"That's how it better be." Esther kissed him back.

Chapter 14

The Case of Miss Applesaucepants

Miss Applegate was in tears again. She taught the Sunday pre-school classes as well as running the pre-school program for the school. Every week she appeared with a new reason for quitting. An only child, she had been home-schooled and secluded from the world by over-protective parents. She had attended a girls-only Christian college and had little experience with real life, including experience with small children.

Her students teased her mercilessly, calling her Miss Applesaucepants. Chants of "Miss Applesaucepants, Miss Applesaucepants," could be heard coming down the hallway to her class. Pre-school children know so well how to latch onto a phrase or word they find funny and repeat and repeat without it losing its appeal to them. Miss Applesaucepants was second only to taunts of poopypants, poopyhead and anything else related to bodily functions.

"You poopyhead," one child would call another and thus the rain of poop-related repartees would begin.

"You're a poopyhead!"

"You've got poopypants!"

"You poopyface!" The chorus would ensue with the laughter growing and growing with each taunt.

Miss Applegate came to see Pastor K for her weekly pep talks, usually in tears.

"What's the matter, Trina?" I asked. I was on first name basis with Miss Applegate.

"Those children ..." she started.

"What did they do this time?" I asked, anticipating another hysterical story to share with my friends over coffee. Pre-school kids were the best.

"What didn't they do?" Miss Applegate responded.

"I know. It's always something, isn't it?"

"Yes," Trina reached for a tissue and blew her nose. "You know how the children insist on calling me Miss Applesaucepants? And how they love to use the word poopy?"

The young girl shifted uncomfortably in the chair, waiting to see the pastor. She appeared to be in her early teens, thin and unusually graceful for someone at that age. Marcie recognized what she had so lacked when she had been the same age.

"I'll be back to pick you up in an hour," the girl's mom said. At least that was who Marcie thought the woman was. Marcie thought she recognized the girl. Wasn't she one of the Reese kids? If so, then that wasn't her mother, but the stepmom, Ava. Ava seemed nice, for a stepmom. Marcie felt a twinge of jealousy. If only she had had such a stepmom.

"The pastor is running a little late," Marcie told the girl. "He should be here soon. Can I get you anything? Water, pop?" They had a store of pop in the kitchenette off of her office.

"No," the girl fidgeted, then added, "Thank you."

"Are you Ashley Reese?" Marcie broke the awkward silence.

"Yes," was the monosyllabic response.

"I knew your mom. I took dance lessons from her when I was younger."

"Oh." Ashley continued to fidget, picking up a magazine as a distraction. "My dad and stepmom think I need to talk to the pastor." Ashley put the magazine down.

"Why?"

"Because of my mom. It's more my stepmom than my dad. Says I'm not coping."

"Are you? Not coping, that is."

"They don't understand. No one understands. I'm not a little kid. I don't fit in with the kids at school."

"Growing up without a mom you do feel different."

"How would you know?"

"My mom died when I was little. I never knew her. It was just me and my dad. You have a stepmom, and a brother and a sister. I only have my dad."

"It doesn't matter. They don't understand. My friends don't understand."

"I had two good friends growing up," Marcie added.

"Two more than me."

Marcie didn't know what else to say. Why didn't Pastor Joe hurry up, she thought, hoping to end this conversation.

"I'm older than other kids my age," Ashley continued.

"I know. I felt that too. You grow up quick when you don't have a mom. I had to do a lot of things for myself, stuff a mom would have done. Dad was okay, but he wasn't Mom."

"Kids my age are so immature." Marcie nodded her head in agreement to what Ashley had said. "The older girls don't want anything to do with me."

Marcie could relate but wasn't sure what to say. "Guess I was lucky to have my friends."

"You were."

"At least you knew your mom. I never knew my mom. She died when I was a baby."

"You didn't have to watch your mom be sick and die from cancer."

"No, I didn't." Marcie agreed with Ashley. She didn't know who had it worse. Perhaps her fantasies about caring for someone with cancer were just that, unreal, made up. She imagined the real thing was not so pleasant.

Marcie was relieved when Pastor Joe walked through the door.

"So sorry to be late," he told Ashley as he escorted her to his office. "I hope Marcie has been keeping you company."

Ashley didn't say anything as she walked into the pastor's office. She looked back over her shoulder at Marcie as if to say, "Get me out of here."

Marcie waved to her through the window of Pastor Joe's office door.

Chapter 15

Even though St. Luke's was not big, it seemed there was a steady stream of visitors to the church office. Pastor Joe was becoming well known among the residents of Cascade Falls for his kindness and sage advice. Each person came with their own story to tell. Pastor Joe had infinite patience for the foibles of those woe-begotten souls. Catholics visited from St. Paul's across town, to make confessions in the safety of his office. Baptists and Episcopalians made their way to his door, as well as those "nones" – people of no particular faith background in the census. He particularly enjoyed chatting with them, not because he was out to convert them, but because he found them to be more spiritually honest than many of the church goers he knew. Perhaps that was part of what attracted him to Kathleen. He found her honesty refreshing; her bad girl attitude intriguing. He wouldn't change her for the world.

"I can always find women ready to agree with me and tell me how wonderful I am," he had told her once. "It's rare to find someone willing to let me know when I'm full of ... you know what."

"So, I'm a rare bird?"

"You might say that."

"Don't try to cage me or domesticate me, or I'll be gone."

"Never. I'll never do that. I need your honesty in my life. Church members put their ministers on pedestals. Otherwise I might get sucked into believing it myself."

"No fear of that with me around."

Yes, Kathleen was refreshing. Still he kept her at arm's length, not quite ready to let his congregation know about her. Kathleen seemed to like it better that way too.

If only they had the money to pay better and hire a real secretary, he wished. But they didn't and he was stuck with this twentysomething, flitter bug, who dashed off after the least little distraction.

Joe sat down with Kathleen to the home-cooked meal he had prepared. Cooking wasn't Kathleen's forte. She did make attempts to keep up her end of providing meals to share, though Joe suspected some of those meals were prepared by Kathleen's mother. Some things are best not looked into too deeply. He took the meals and enjoyed them without question. Tonight, it was his turn. They did go out to eat at times, but he preferred eating in the privacy of their respective homes, away from the prying eyes of his church members. Their relationship was as much a secret to him as it was to his church members. He wasn't sure exactly where it was going, but he was along for the ride. Kathleen continued to be a mystery to him, a mystery he was content to explore and possibly take a lifetime to solve. He knew about her history, her time in prison, but he also knew she had since cleaned up her act. Still there were depths to her that he couldn't begin to know. He liked it that way. Some secrets are not meant to be known. Theirs was a sweet secret, a relationship he wanted to keep to himself for as long as he could.

"So, how goes it with your new secretary?" Kathleen asked. Joe's struggle to find the right secretary was a common conversation topic.

"Well, at least she's not sneaking off to the coffee shop anymore."

"At least." Kathleen smiled as she cut the chicken breast on her plate.

"Why? What do you know? What's going on now?"

Kathleen slowly chewed her chicken before answering, relishing the moment and holding Joe in suspense. "It seems she's writing a blog."

"A blog?"

"Yes, a live journal, on-line, posted so anyone can read it."

"I know what a blog is."

"Have you seen hers?"

"I have better things to do with my time than read my secretary's journal."

"I think maybe you ought to." Kathleen tapped on her phone a few times then handed it to Joe. "Here, check out her latest post."

Joe looked at the small screen at a website entitled, *Delicious Secrets.* Under the title were the words – *What are your most tantalizing secrets?* He looked over at Kathleen.

"Keep reading."

Who's the raven haired buxom beauty calling the Pastor each day? Clearly she has some secret worth hiding. Perhaps another life, a secret life on stage in off-Broadway productions. Having never made it as an actress, she is resigned to a life of obscurity running a school of dance, sending others off for the acclaim she herself was unable to achieve. And what is the hold this temptress has on the middle-aged Pastor? Is she out to entrap the most eligible bachelor in town?

"What is this? Where does she come up with this stuff?"

"It gets better. You should read some of the parts about your church members. She changes the names and some of their features, but, hey, this is a small community. It's easy to figure out who she's talking about."

Joe glanced through some of the posts. "So, is this what she is doing on her computer all the time? Every time I come into the office she shuts it. She thinks I don't see, but I know she's been on her laptop instead of working."

"It appears to be. I've never been referred to as a raven-haired buxom beauty before. I kind of like it."

"Does anyone actually read this?"

"Just all the teen girls at the Dance Studio. That's how I found out. They love her posts."

Joe shook his head as he tried to figure out what to do. "It doesn't say who is writing the blog. How do we know it's her? How do we know it's not some secretary at some other church in ... New Hampshire or New Jersey?"

"Here," Kathleen swiped her finger over the phone screen a few times, "read this."

Cascades is a small city in the middle of nowhere where I grew up and where I continue to live out a life of servitude as a church secretary, awaiting my opportunity to escape from its mundane existence. In the meantime, I'm stuck spending my days privy to the comings and goings of an array of spinsters, pan-handlers, mothers with puking infants, and doddering dolts who make up the congregation of the Church of St. Everybody.

"Okay, I got it. It's her."

"Read on," Kathleen finished off her plate while Joe read the blog posts.

The pastor, my boss, is a widower with two grown daughters. He, more than anyone, has more than his share of secrets that he is keeping from his faithful flock. It shall be my quest to uncover these secrets and others within the posts of this blog.

"Who else could it be but her?"

"I guess I better talk to her."

"You guess?" Kathleen took her phone back from him and leaned back. "What's for dessert?"

Chapter 16

What was that? Marcie saw something hanging from the electrical wiring in the middle of the street on her way to work. How had it gotten there? Why hadn't she noticed it before? It dangled like it was daring her, daring her to climb up and take a look. As she got closer, she realized it was a pair of shoes, sneakers it appeared, tied together by a shoe lace and hanging on either side of the wire. Someone must have thrown them up there, but who? And why? She stopped her bike, pulled out her phone and took a picture. Something to put in my blog, she thought as she rode the rest of the way to work.

The Case of the Dangling Tennis Shoes.

The latest mystery to come to my attention is the mystery of the dangling tennis shoes. These shoes are now hanging high above Maple Street between Second and Third, hanging from the wire that crisscrosses the street. Who threw them and left them to entertain passersby? Perhaps a disgruntled runner, tired of running away from his problems, tossed them to show he would never run again? Or perhaps they were the shoes of some erstwhile lovers, tossed in anger after a break-up? Or someone showing off, tossing the shoes over the wire, not expecting them to become firmly lodged. Perhaps they tried to knock them down by throwing stones at the shoes or tried to find a pole long enough to prod one shoe over the wire, all to no avail. Perhaps there is an urchin running barefoot in the street even as you read this, afraid to go home without his or her shoes out of fear of the punishment that might await them. Or perhaps it was some callous teen who had shoes a-plenty. What was one pair donated to the wire god above?

Help me solve this mystery. If any of you know the shoes' owner and how they came to be there, I would love to know.

SS

There, Marcie thought as she sent the post on the internet for all to see. Certainly, someone would know. And if not, she could keep blogging about them. She shut her laptop as Pastor Joe approached.

"Marcie, I need to talk to you. In my office," he stated. "And bring your laptop," he added as she started to get up.

"What's this about, chief?" Marcie sat down in the chair across from his desk, her usual spot, one she was getting used to as she had multiple meetings with the pastor. Pastor Joe remained standing.

"Why is it, you close your laptop every time I come into the office? What are you hiding?"

"Nothing, boss, er Pastor."

Pastor Joe continued to stand, staring down at her from his full height. "Then let me see it."

"It's private, girl stuff. Nothing that would interest you."

"Is that so? It wouldn't have anything to do with a blog called, '*Delicious Secrets*,' would it?"

Marcie shifted in her seat. "Busted," she heard the voice in her left-brain whisper. She glanced at the door as if about to make a run for it. Pastor Joe blocked her way.

"I've already seen it, Marcie. I know what's on the site. Did you write it?"

"Yes," Marcie slowly looked up as she said the word. Pastor Joe pulled a chair alongside of hers, sat down and looked across at her rather than hovering over her.

"I'm glad you told the truth." He paused as he plotted his words. "Do you understand the role of secretary? It's a position of trust. You are privy to the comings and goings of all the people coming to this church seeking assistance, seeking comfort, seeking guidance. They need to know that this is a safe place where what they say and do is confidential."

"I didn't use anyone's real names. I made stuff up. What harm is there in that?"

"Really, Marcie, Mrs. MoneyBags, Mr. and Mrs. Two-timers, and Miss Poopysauce. What were you thinking?" Marcie fought the nervous laughter sliding up her throat and into her mouth. She caught it behind her teeth, not daring to look at Pastor lest it slip out. "And Pastor Knowitall and the buxom Ms. Blossom?"

"It was all in jest, for a laugh."

"People reading your blog may think what you are writing is true. It's not hard to guess who you are referring to. You have a sacred trust and you have violated that trust."

"I'm sorry, Pastor." Marcie looked down at the computer in her lap. "Am I fired?" Pastor Joe got up and went around the desk to his chair.

"No, you're not fired. What I want you to do is reflect on what it means to be a secretary. Here are some Scripture references to secretaries. I want you to read them, think about them, and then tell me what you think. It's a noble profession, one not to be taken lightly." Joe reached across the desk and handed Marcie a slip of paper. "Now get out of here, get back to work."

Marcie started to get up when he stopped her. "Oh, and take down that website."

"What if I write about something else? It just gets so boring some days."

"I realize it can be a boring job, especially when you have all of your work done. Why don't you do some research on-line, find something more meaningful to write about? There's so much going on in the world. You said you want your life to have meaning. Once you have your work done, you can read the news, but not those fake sites. Go to reputable sites, credible news sources. If you have any question just ask me. You could write about that, but no more writing about church members."

"Yes, boss, er Pastor," Marcie moved towards the door then stopped. "Pastor?"

Pastor Joe looked up from his desk where he had already started to go over his messages, moving on to other responsibilities.

"You won't tell my dad, will you?"

"No, Marcie," Pastor Joe stared at her as he considered options. Marcie waited as he sighed and shook his head. "It will be our secret. Now get out of here so I can get some work done."

Marcie's step felt lighter as she left the office. Not only was she not fired, she had just been given the go ahead to surf the web while at work. It wasn't such a bad day, or a bad job after all.

Chapter 17

"Let me get this straight. Not only did you not get fired, he actually said it was okay to go on the internet while at work?"

"As long as my work's done. There isn't a lot going on during the summer, especially now that Bible school is over. I thought he would pile on busy work."

"My mom was a secretary once. She never had any free time at work, at least not from what she said. Certainly didn't have time to surf the web. She always had more work than time."

"Maybe she's just wasn't as fast as I am."

"My mom? You're talking about my mom, you know." Marcie knew. If anything, Gwen's mom could type and file circles around her, even on her bad days. "No, you're just lucky you have such a good boss."

"You try working for him."

"I would. Pastor Joe is a sweetheart."

"Why, Gwen, do you have a crush on the good pastor?"

"And if I did, what would it hurt? I wouldn't be the first church member to drool a little over the Pastor. He's dreamy. And there's something just a little dark and mysterious about him. Just like you wrote in your blog."

"I was making that up. Besides, he's old enough to be your father." Marcie was beginning to wonder if Pastor Joe had been right about the negative influence of her blog. "And he has a girlfriend."

"Oh, her. I hate her. She doesn't deserve him. And besides, they aren't really going out, not publicly. I think it's all made up by you. He's not dating anyone and therefore he's fair game."

"You believe what you want to believe, but I tell you, he's not available."

"I will believe what I want to believe."

Marcie looked at Mei-Lin, quietly applying lacquer to Marcie's finger nails. She seemed even quieter than usual, if that was possible. Marcie noticed bruises on her arm, just above the line of her short sleeve shirt. It was hard to see but she was able to get a glance depending on how Mei-Lin moved her arm. It looked as if someone had grabbed her by the arm and squeezed their fingers into her skin, not breaking the skin but hard enough to leave a mark. Mei-Lin was so skinny. There was little fat or muscle that Marcie could see. It wouldn't take much to leave a mark. Marcie knew who she suspected. She looked over at the owner, chatting with another customer. Marcie looked away lest the owner suspect that Marcie knew what she had done.

Marcie smiled at Mei-Lin as she finished applying the final coat. Mei-Lin didn't smile back. When Marcie tried to sneak a few dollars into her hand, she refused, saying no and pointing to the tip jar. Marcie wondered if the other girls would have been so insistent. The two other girls laughed and chatted with each other, ignoring Mei-Lin most of the time. Marcie wished she could speak to Mei-Lin alone but saw no chance of that. It seemed Mei-Lin's whole life was confined within the walls of the nail salon.

"Did you see the bruises on Mei-Lin's arm?" Marcie asked once they got outside.

"No, and you better not. Don't ruin a good thing by sticking your nose in other people's business and making up stories. You got away with it once, but that was with the pastor. He had to forgive you. You're a church member."

"My dad's the church member, not me."

"Whatever. I don't think Mei-Lin's boss would be the forgiving type. You want to get coffee?"

"No, I'm meeting Bernie. We're going for a bike ride." Marcie straddled her bike.

"You and Bernie. You're quite the item again."

"What do you mean again?"

"I mean, again. You were an item in high school and you are one now."

"We weren't going out in high school. We were just friends."

"You call it what you want. That's not how I saw it."

"We went out with other people."

"Yes, but I always saw through that. I could tell there was something going on."

"Then you knew more than I knew."

"And what about that kiss at the prom."

"It was just one kiss. Then he was gone."

"You believe what you want, and I'll believe what I know." Marcie refused to respond as she rode away on her bike. Yes, it was just one kiss, but what a kiss ...

Chapter 18

Fake News is No News

What is all this about fake news? I don't get it. Every time you disagree with a news report, you claim it's fake, right? Meanwhile anyone and everyone can start a blog and become an overnight expert on their subject, whether they are or not. Something's not right there. Who is doing the fact checking and solid investigation when so many journalists are losing jobs as newspapers across the country cut staff positions or close completely?

The more we know, the more we realize how little we know. There's so much information at our fingertips through the internet, and less trust of formerly considered respectable news sources. Who are we to believe? Where does one find truth?

I'd love to hear your thoughts on fake news. What is it? Who determines this? Is it better to have no news than fake news? Write me!

SS

"Since when did you start writing about fake news?" Henry, Marcie's dad, put down his paper as Marcie came in. "I didn't think you were interested in any kind of news."

"Since when did you start reading my blog?" Marcie responded.

"You'd be surprised how much I read, not just what's in the newspaper or magazines. This is a change from what you usually write."

"Oh, that," Marcie sat down across from her dad as she figured out how much to tell him.

"Yes, this is a far cry from the Church of St. Everybody."

"You know about that too."

"Yes, I do."

Marcie looked away from her dad before answering. "I guess I got carried away. I was having so much fun. But Pastor didn't see it that way."

"I would think not. Did he fire you?"

"No, actually he didn't. He just told me I couldn't write about church members anymore. He was the one who suggested I write, what he called, more substantial posts. What do you think?"

"I look forward to seeing what else you have to write about. Are you getting any response from your readers?"

"Not yet, but this was the first new post. I'll probably lose followers, but that's okay."

"Better that than to lose your job."

"I guess," Marcie got up and excused herself. She had just been starting to have fun with the blog. Now she had to change it. Not that she was the first person to change direction after starting a blog. She knew she would lose followers. You always do when you don't give people what they expect. Still, it was interesting reading the news, looking for noteworthy, or blog-worthy, topics. Pastor Joe had given her a number of think tanks that he recommended: the Brookings Institute, Human Rights Watch and the Council on Foreign Relations. She found others on-line. Who would have thought there were so many think tanks where people were paid just to read, think, discuss and write about issues affecting humans? It's amazing how much she didn't know. It did cut into her fun time, but she didn't miss it.

She went for a week before launching her new venture. She wanted to give herself time to have something to write about now that she wasn't just making it up as she went. She didn't even mind it when people asked her about the Church of St. Everybody and complained.

I'm taking the blog in a new direction. I hope you will come along with me. She posted.

Chapter 19

"Write about me in your blog," Ashley said. She had started coming early to her appointments with Pastor Joe in order to have time to talk to Marcie. Now that school was out, she rode her bike to the church office, always arriving ten to fifteen minutes early.

"What blog?" Marcie looked sideways at Ashley, trying to figure out how much she knew.

"You know what blog. It's all anybody talks about."

She's got me, Marcie thought before replying. "Pastor Joe has told me I can't write about church members anymore."

"I'll talk to Pastor Joe."

"Okay. If you get Pastor Joe's okay."

"What name will you give me?"

"I don't know. Haven't thought about it." Marcie thought. "How about Miss Precocious?"

Ashley considered the option, seeming to swirl it around in her head and taste it on her lips. "Maybe. I'll think about it. How will you describe me?"

"That's easy, a skinny twelve-year-old with a long blond ponytail and wisdom beyond her years."

"That's okay."

"Good, now let me get back to my work."

Ashley and Pastor Joe had come to an agreement that first appointment. At first Ashley had sat for a long time without saying anything. Pastor Joe had waited patiently until she finally spoke up.

"This was my dad and stepmom's idea, not mine."

"I know," Pastor Joe answered.

"They think I'm depressed or something." Ashley sat with her legs crossed tightly in front of her.

"Are you? Depressed or something?"

"No, I wish everyone would stop thinking I am."

"Why do they think you are depressed?"

"Because I don't want to do anything with the family."

"Sounds pretty normal for a teen to me."

"They say I'm angry all the time."

"Are you angry?"

"Yes, at them." Ashley re-crossed her legs.

"I guess I would be angry too, if I were you."

"I'm not crazy."

"No, you aren't."

"Then why do I have to come see you?"

"Well, Ashley, you can look at this several ways. I know you are not crazy, and you know you are not crazy. You could go on being angry at your parents."

"Dad and stepmom," Ashley interrupted.

"Dad and stepmom, or you could humor them. Come here and see me and maybe they'll get off your back."

"What will we do when I'm here?"

"We can do whatever you want to do. It's up to you. We could play video games if you like."

"Nah, I don't like video games." Ashley looked over at Pastor Joe. "I don't need a counselor."

"Then how about we be friends?"

"And I don't need a new mom."

"I was friends with your mom, especially the last years of her life."

"I know. I remember you visiting. What did you talk about, you and my mom?"

"Lots of stuff, but that was between us, just like what we talk about will be between you and me."

"Our secret?"

"Yes, I guess. If you want to call it that." Pastor Joe leaned forward in his chair. "It was no secret how your mom felt about you. She loved you very much."

"I know." Ashley slouched angrily at the suggestion.

"And she worried about you and your brother and sister, and your dad, too."

"She didn't need to worry about Dad. He's got Ava. She didn't need to worry about me. I take care of myself."

"She's a mom. She had to worry. It's what parents do."

"If I agree to come back, what will you tell my dad?"

"Not much. Just that we talked. You can trust that no one will know what we talk about. It will be between us."

"And we don't have to talk about anything in particular?"

"We'll only talk about what you want to talk about."

"Won't everybody think something's wrong with me if they know I am seeing you?"

"No one will know but you, me, your parents and Marcie, the secretary. You can just sit here and read if you want."

"I know about you and Aunt Kathleen." Ashley uncrossed her legs and leaned back.

"I promise I won't tell your aunt anything either."

"That's okay. I like Aunt Kathleen. You can tell her what you want." Ashley thought a while longer. "Okay," she finally agreed. "I guess so." That had been her first appointment. Pastor Joe had been surprised when Ashley told him about wanting to be in Marcie's blog.

"But I thought you didn't want anyone to know we were meeting."

"If she writes about me in her blog, then Janene and the others will take me more seriously."

"So, is that what this is about? Being accepted by the older girls at the Dance Studio?"

"They think I'm too young to notice. I don't fit in with the girls my age."

"You always have been mature for your age. Dealing with death can do that to a person, make them wise beyond their years."

"The other kids don't get it. Maybe the older girls will."

"Maybe, but maybe not. Being mature doesn't depend on being older." Pastor paused, "It's hard feeling alone."

"How can I feel alone with Grace always tagging along? I have to share my bedroom with her."

"And yet you feel alone."

"You said I didn't have to talk about anything I didn't want to."

"Yes, I did."

"I don't want to talk about this. Can Marcie write about me in her blog?"

"It's entirely up to you," Pastor Joe agreed.

"Good," Ashley stood up. "I'm ready to go now."

On her way out after her appointment with Pastor Joe, Ashley told Marcie she had the go ahead to write about her.

"I'll check with Pastor Joe," Marcie said. She wasn't going to lose her job because of a twelve-year-old.

"I can't wait to see what you write," Ashley said as she went out the door.

"It's up to Ashley," Pastor Joe told Marcie when she asked him. "Oh, by the way, I have someone to help you with the bulletin each week. Ashley."

"What are you talking about? I don't need help with the bulletin. There's hardly enough work to keep me busy. Why do I need a helper?" Running copies, stuffing and folding the bulletin for the Sunday Service took all of two hours, if that much. Marcie could do it in her sleep.

"Maybe you don't need the help, but Ashley could use a friend. Besides, you said you wanted to do something that was meaningful. What is more meaningful than helping a young girl without a mother? It will be good for you."

Marcie could see there was no point in arguing. Just what she didn't need. A twelve-year-old to take care of. Marcie sighed and opened her laptop.

Chapter 20

They were riding on the bike trail that had been made from an old railroad track. Marcie enjoyed thinking about all the people who had once ridden along the tracks in the trains. She imagined hobos, jumping into box cars; young men riding the rails in search of adventure, joining the ranks of the hobos. And then there were the Pullman porters, escorting paying passengers to their seats, celebrities riding from Detroit to Chicago, two hot spots of the time.

"Do you realize that Detroit was once the fifth largest city in the country? That puts it up there with cities like Denver, Los Angeles, Washington D.C., Chicago. That was before the riots of '67 and white flight to the suburbs. I wonder what would have happened if there had not been the riots or if the whites hadn't left. I wonder if Detroit would have remained in the top five cities."

"That was before my time," Bernie commented.

"Mine too, but it's good to know this stuff."

"Is it? I'm beginning to think that pastor doesn't know what he's doing, encouraging you to read all this stuff on-line. A little knowledge can be dangerous." Bernie looked over at her and smiled, inviting her to take him on. Marcie avoided his grin as she kept her eyes on the path ahead of her, but she knew the invitation.

"And a lot of ignorance is clearly dangerous. That's what we have right now. We have the whole world at our fingertips through the web, yet people choose to live in ignorance, surrounding themselves with people who think the same way they do, reading only that which they agree with, ignoring anything that might challenge them or, God forbid, lead them to change their way of thinking. Ignorance – to ignore anything or anyone that doesn't agree with you. That's my definition."

"What's the big deal?"

"It's what I've been reading."

"Or maybe who has gotten to you, putting all these ideas in your head. Do I need to be jealous of this pastor?"

"That's ridiculous. He's my dad's age."

"Lots of women your age with daddy issues work them out with older men."

"I don't have daddy issues. I have mommy issues, like you."

"I have both."

"That we can agree on." Marcie picked up speed, pulling ahead of Bernie as they approached the point in the path where they could see the lake. Bernie struggled to keep up on the dirt bike he had bought for the summer. Not ideal for riding on pavement, though great if they chose to go off the road. Marcie's thin tires sped easily on the path, leaving him behind.

Marcie loved the way the lake just appeared, as if out of nowhere, and then, all of a sudden, there was water on both sides of the path. The first time she had ridden this path, she had been feeling down. She had gone through an area of darkness where the trees completely covered the path, then was surprised by the patch of blue appearing to her right. She had known there was a lake somewhere along the path, just didn't know where. And then, when she saw the lake on both sides and sunlight sending rays of sparkles off the lake, her spirits had lifted. She knew then, that everything would be all right. That had been the summer after Bernie had left.

"Another beautiful day," Marcie said to herself as she pulled up to a bench overlooking the lake. "Time for a break," she told Bernie as he caught up. "I always stop here before riding back to town. I like looking out over the lake. It helps me when I'm feeling down."

Marcie walked to the edge of the overlook at the water a short distance below. Bernie came up behind her and wrapped his arms around her.

"You aren't feeling down now, are you?"

"No, not at all." Marcie gazed across the expanse of the lake to the other side. "I used to come here a lot that summer after you left."

"I'm sorry about that."

"No need to be sorry anymore. That's in the past." She glanced to the side and saw what appeared to be a hammock hanging between two trees and zippered shut. It hung like a cocoon between the branches.

"Bernie, look," she whispered, nodding in the direction of the hammock. "It looks like someone's in there."

Beside another tree was a small backpack, next to the backpack a box of cinnamon sugar Pop-tarts, a bottle of vitamin water and a bottle of Mountain Dew.

"Not exactly a health nut," Marcie indicated the backpack. Next to the backpack was a girl's Hello Kitty bike, painted black though with a pink seat and handle bars.

"Do you think it's a little girl? That's a little girl's bike," Marcie whispered.

"If it was, would she really be out here alone, sleeping in a hammock?"

"Then who? Maybe it's a runaway?"

"Now don't let that beautiful imagination of yours runaway with you."

"We could wait and see who got out."

"Or we could ride back and get something to eat. I'm in favor of food."

"You always are."

"Come on." Bernie refused to let go of his grip around her waist. "Leave it alone. Don't go looking for trouble. If you want trouble, I'm sure I could stir some up for you."

"That you could." Marcie agreed to drive back to town, but didn't forget the hammock. "Maybe the bike is stolen, stolen from some little girl," she said over hamburgers.

"What bike?"

"The Hello Kitty bike. Don't you pay attention? Have you forgotten already?"

"Clearly you haven't. I thought you were going to let it go."

"You were going to let it go. I only agreed to ride back so you could feed that insatiable stomach of yours."

"There's something else that's insatiable." Bernie grinned when Marcie laughed. He figured he had diverted her attention momentarily but knew he hadn't heard the end of it yet.

Chapter 21

Coffee – Health Drink or Death's Elixir?

Following my post on fake news, I've been thinking about all of the conflicting health information on the web. Case in point and one close to my heart: the lowly coffee bean. I drink my coffee plain, au lait (with milk), as espresso in lattes and sugared up for a dessert. My favorite – caramel machiatto. Perhaps you can relate.

In return for my devotion to this beverage, I get more conflicting reports than Starbucks has flavors. Some tout coffee as a health food, giving us a natural jolt in the morning to jump start our day, staving off dementia in the elderly. Others claim that not only is there no health benefit, it may cause harm, jiving up jittery nerves, frazzling already frenzied minds, leading to confusion and an inability to focus, taxing hearts, leading to arrhythmia.

If you don't like the latest findings, wait a day. There will be new findings tomorrow. You can pretty much find information on the internet to support whatever you want to believe.

As for me, I'll not be giving up my coffee any time soon.

Again, I ask, in this world of fake news and conflicting information, where can one find truth? It's a secret I hope to uncover.

SS

"Pastor, did you hear about the immigrants that died in that truck in Arizona?" Marcie caught Joe before he could make it to the confines of his office. It seemed everyday Marcie had something new she wanted to talk to him about. He had liked it better when she had avoided him. Then he had been able to get to the work at hand without any unnecessary chitchat. Now it seemed that she was ever waiting for his arrival to share the latest news from the internet. When did she find time to do her work?

"Have you already filled out that report for me?"

"Did it yesterday. Here it is." Marcie handed him the report. "You know, I don't just go on-line while I'm here. Most of the stuff I ask about I read at home or during my lunch break."

"Yes, well ..." How did she know I was wondering about that? "Yes, it's terrible. It appears they were being trafficked."

"I've been reading about human trafficking. Here I thought slavery had ended with the Civil War. I'm glad we don't have that problem here."

"Don't we?"

"Why no, we don't have any trafficking in Cascade Falls. That only happens in big cities."

"Do your research. We are on the I-94 corridor from Detroit to Chicago. What better place for drug trafficking, and other trafficking?"

"But not in Cascade Falls."

"If you say so." Joe was impatient to get to his office. Marcie stopped him again before he could get out the door.

"Pastor, you haven't heard anything about a runaway, have you?"

"No, why do you ask?

"I was riding to Otter Lake. When I got there I saw one of those enclosed hammocks. You know the kind, zipper ..."

"Yes, I know. Get on with it."

"Well, someone was sleeping in it and next to it was a backpack and a Hello Kitty bike. I thought maybe someone had run away."

"Don't you think that if it was a runaway, they wouldn't have been sleeping in a place where they could be seen so easily?"

"I guess not. Still, doesn't it seem suspicious?"

"I'll let you know if I hear anything." Joe finally made it out of the front office to his office. He was pleased that Marcie was no longer writing about him or church members. He had started reading her blog to ensure that did not happen again. He hadn't wanted to but figured he had to. Yet another responsibility in the never-ending tasks that are required of a pastor, he thought as he turned on his computer. Wasn't it enough that he had to meet with her once a week to check on her progress and assign work? He hadn't had to do that with Edna. Edna had been there longer than he had been. She knew more about the goings-on of the church than he did. She had been self-motivated and self-directed, never needing much support from him. Often, she was the one telling him what needed doing and giving him the support he needed to keep the church going. She had been the ideal secretary. He was looking for that again. Would he ever find it?

"Probably about the time she knows what she's doing, she'll be gone," he had thought to himself. When he had asked her about her thoughts on the Scripture passages he had given her, he had been surprised. She had actually put some thought into it, but not the thoughts he had hoped for.

"I read those passages you wanted me to read," Marcie told him.

"And ..."

"Well, yes, secretaries were important back then, but that was before everyone knew how to read and write. It was a profession requiring specific training and skills not available to everyone. Not like today. Everybody can read and write and use a computer now. It's nothing special."

"But not everyone is proficient at those skills. Not everyone can be a good secretary."

"If you say so." Marcie agreed with him, but it wasn't the victory he was looking for. Marcie had chosen not to fight.

Chapter 22

Little Miss Precocious floated into the pastor's office, her hair tucked into a tasteful bun, and landed in a chair after a graceful pirouette. At twelve, she exuded the grace of a twenty-year-old —

"Hmmm, I like that," Ashley said as she read over Marcie's shoulder. "That will show Janene."

—and a wisdom beyond her years. She was meeting with Pastor K once a week at her parents' behest. As is so often the case with teens, she was the designated problem, hiding the real source of problems in the family, which always rested with the parents. When teens act up and end up in counseling, it is usually because of some other problem that has been superimposed on the teen from the parents.

"What does that mean?"

"That the teen acts out because of the parents' problems."

"I don't know ..." Ashley scrunched her face as she thought.

"It's all made up. What does it matter?"

"How about something like, she's so far above others of her age, that her parents, who are normal human beings, think there is something wrong with her."

"I can work with that," Marcie started to type again.

Being precocious for her age since she was little, she was always misunderstood. When she wrote the works of Shakespeare using blocks in kindergarten, her teacher took away her blocks. In grade school she read Beowulf and Chaucer while others were reading Harry Potter. Now, in middle school, she was devouring the works of Tolstoy and Dostoevsky in their original Russian.

"How's that?" Marcie stopped typing.

"Okay, except I have no idea what you are talking about."

"How about you tell me what you want me to write." Clearly there was a reason why writers wrote alone, Marcie thought as she waited for this advanced preteen to tell her what she wanted.

"I want it to be something Janene and the others would like."

"So, tell me about them. What do they talk about?"

"Your blog."

"What else?"

"Well, boys, school dances, high school stuff."

"So how about we put you into high school?"

"Okay," Ashley agreed.

Marcie sighed as she started writing again.

Miss Precocious was a lithe young dancer with her hair pulled back into a bun and an acumen for life that was far beyond her years. She had moved up the ranks of her classmates, surpassing them as easily as playing the board game, "Go to the Head of the Class," until she found herself, at the tender age of twelve, in her junior year of high school.

Her grace as a dancer surpassed all others and made her a sought-after partner on the dance floor. Her witticisms entranced all those she encountered. So why was she seeing Pastor K on a weekly basis?

Because she was so far beyond all others of her age that it was assumed there must be a problem. And so, she was sent to see Pastor K so that he could rob her of her originality and unique perspective and become what she was not: an ordinary teenager. For you see, Miss Precocious was far from ordinary, however only she and I knew that. It was our secret as she met with the pastor and pretended to be impressed by what he had to say until he finally pronounced her cured and ready for normal society.

But Miss Precocious and I knew differently.

SS

Marcie posted it that night.

"What did you think of my post?" she asked Ashley when she saw that Friday.

"It was good, only you didn't mention that I play guitar. Did you know I play guitar?" Ashley proceeded to fill Marcie in on her guitar playing while she folded bulletins.

Chapter 23

"I hear that Bernie Rogers is back in town." Marcie's dad put down his newspaper as she came through the door.

"Oh, you do?" Marcie slipped onto the couch, feigning nonchalance.

"Yes, I do. I spoke with his grandmother today."

"That's nice." Marcie picked up a section of the newspaper and pretended to read.

"She said you were dating again."

"Well, you know her. You can't trust what she says. She's ancient, doesn't remember what she has to eat for breakfast, much less what her grandson is doing. She's probably confusing now with back when he was in high school."

"Is she now? That's funny, because she seems to have her wits about her every time I talk to her."

"Well, she's good at hiding it. You know how some old people are."

"And how would you know that? How would you know what Bernie's grandmother remembers and doesn't remember?"

"Well, I ... she comes to the church office all the time ... You know how those old women are."

"Yes, and I know you. I know when you are lying. What's the secrecy about? I knew you were seeing someone. Why try to hide it from me? Bernie's a fine young man. I always liked him."

"I know, Dad. It's just, I thought you might be upset or tell me he wasn't good enough for me, remind me about how he had left back in high school."

"Was that me you were afraid would say that, or you saying it to yourself?"

"Dad ..." Marcie put down the paper and looked at her dad.

"I do remember how much he hurt you when he left in such a hurry. A father doesn't forget when his little girl is hurt. And yes, he did get into trouble a lot when he was in high school, but if you knew his family as I did, you'd understood why. Not that I necessarily wanted my only daughter involved with such a family. Still Bernie seemed all right, was always polite when we talked and he cared about you. He wasn't good enough for you, of course. No one is good enough for my little girl."

"All right, Dad. I get it. Everything I said you would say."

"I didn't say that."

"Yes, you did, in your own way."

"I don't want you to be hurt again."

"I know, Dad. I don't want to be hurt either, but if I do, it's my choice."

"I wish I could save you from all of the unpleasantness of life."

"I know, Dad, but you can't."

"Can't blame a dad for trying."

"Well, I'll forgive you anyway."

"That's my girl." Henry picked the paper back up. "Bernie's grandma said he was just staying for a few weeks." Marcie heard his voice from behind the paper.

"That's right, Dad. He has to go back to Tennessee in August."

"Said something about him being in a band."

"Again, I know, Dad. Is there anything else you want to know?"

"Yes, when are you going to make me some more cookies? I've been out for over a week now." Marcie laughed, went over and kissed her dad on the forehead.

"I'll make some this weekend. I promise."

"That's my girl." Henry put down the newspaper, pushed back in his recliner and reached for the TV remote while Marcie read the paper.

Chapter 24

Ashley couldn't wait to hear what Janene had to say about her blog post. Ashley was helping out with the others at the summer dance camp they held at the end of June. The older dance students helped with the classes of young students. Ashley was helping Chloe with the fourth and fifth graders.

After the classes had been dismissed, Ashley saw Janene and her friends standing around. Now they'll notice me, she thought.

"Hi," Ashley approached the group.

"Well, if it isn't little Miss Precocious, or should I say, Little Miss Prima Donna," Janene said. The other girls laughed at Janene's cue. "Deigning to speak to us peons, so far below you?"

"What are you talking about?" Ashley asked.

"You know what I'm talking about. The blog. How did you manage to weasel your way into the blog? It's obvious that Miss Precocious is you."

"I don't know what you are talking about." Ashley shifted uncomfortably under Janene's glare. This was not what she had expected.

"Sure you don't. You can't understand us lowly, normal people, can you?" Janene snapped her fingers and started to walk away. "Come on, girls." The others followed.

"What was that about?" Kathleen joined her from where she had been watching.

"Nothing," Shame crept up Ashley's neck into her face.

"Those girls. They are just jealous because you were mentioned in *Delicious Secrets* and they weren't. That's all."

"You know too?" Ashley refused to allow tears of embarrassment to surface. She would not acknowledge any discomfiture, at least not now, not until she could find some place private to hide.

"It's pretty obvious, Ashley."

"It's my fault. I asked Marcie to write about me."

"You put her up to it?"

"Yes." Ashley refused to raise her head to meet Kathleen eyes. "I just want to be accepted."

"By them? They aren't worth it. You are way better than any of them, anytime, anywhere, especially that Janene."

"You're just saying that because you're my aunt."

"Yes, I'm your aunt and I love you. That's more than those girls can say." Kathleen's brain started churning with ideas how to get them back. Ashley knew the look on her aunt's face. "We'll show them. Why don't we get something to eat and plot out our revenge?"

"No, Aunt Kathleen. I don't want revenge. I want to forget the whole thing ever happened."

"You are mature for your age. More mature than I was at your age. You deserve your name, little Miss Precocious." Ashley struggled against the smile she felt creeping to her lips. She preferred her role as the offended. "Now come on, nothing like ice cream to help someone forget the sting of shame," Kathleen added.

"Aunt Kathleen, I'm not a baby. You can't make everything better with ice cream."

"Who said it was for you? I need my hot fudge sundae with pecans sprinkled on top after a day like today. We can eat ice cream and make nasty comments about everybody else, then wash it down with a shake. Are you with me?"

"Okay," Ashley gave in and smiled. "But no shake for me. I want to be able to get up on my toes after the summer."

Chapter 25

"I've got a gig." Marcie could hear the excitement in Bernie's voice.

"What?" Marcie responded.

"A gig, a job."

"I know what a gig is."

"It's not a paying one, but it's a chance to perform. I need the practice."

"Where is this gig?"

"Jack's Bar. The owner is a friend of my grandpa's. Gramps told him about me being in a band. He asked if I would come and play on Saturday night. You will come, won't you?"

"Sure, what else do I have to do on Saturday? My boyfriend is working that night."

"If you play your cards right, you may get to go home with a member of the band."

"Just where is this establishment? I don't recognize the name."

"The east side of town, just off of Michigan Avenue. What's wrong?"

"It's just that isn't exactly a good area of town. I know you haven't lived here for a while, but you should remember that."

"I remember Jack's, used to hang out there with my grandpa. It will be fine. Bring Gwen along with you. And you won't be alone. I'll be there."

"Not all the time."

"Look, if you don't want to come ..."

"No, I'll go. It might be good for me, trying something new, breaking out of my rut."

"That's my girl," Bernie started to hug her. She stiffened in his grip. "What's wrong?"

"It's nothing. It's just, that's what my dad always says. Seems weird coming from you."

"Then how about, that's my woman," he said as he pulled her close.

"Much better."

Marcie still wasn't sure about going to Jack's. Gwen, however, was fine with it. She showed up in her skinny jeans and a leather jacket.

"What's this?" Marcie raised her eyebrows and rubbed the leather of her jacket. "Nice."

"Just what the best-dressed women wear to Jack's. I heard they have karaoke tonight. Maybe we can sing a few tunes after Bernie's set." Gwen looked her up and down. "You wearing that?"

"What's wrong with it?" Marcie looked down at her jeans and low-cut top.

"At least put on a pair of skinny jeans, preferably with sparkles on the rear."

"I don't have any with sparkles."

"I thought as much. I came prepared." Gwen reached into her deep purse and pulled out a pair of jeans. "I think they may be a little small, which makes them perfect. Now you do have a jean jacket, don't you?"

"Why do I feel like we are back in high school?" Marcie slipped on a pair of high heeled sandals.

"Because you have been working at the church office all summer. Time to get out, have some fun." Marcie yelled goodbye to her dad as they ran quickly down the stairs and out the house before her dad could see them or ask where they were going.

"What is it about being at home that makes you fall back into all of your old habits?" Marcie commented as they ran down the back steps and climbed into Gwen's car.

The bar was a seedy one as Marcie had feared. "If my dad knew I was here, he would freak," she told Gwen as they scanned the dark establishment.

"That's why he doesn't know. I never tell my parents where I'm going."

"And they're okay with that?"

"Oh, they don't know. I always tell them some place, just never where I'm really going."

The room was empty except for a few men at the bar. They took a table to one side of the area where they saw a microphone. "That must be where Bernie will be performing." Marcie pointed to the mike. "Not much of a stage," she commented. It was just an area of the bar that had been cleared of tables to make space. They were close enough to see Bernie when he played, but not out in the open where they could be seen by others.

"What are you having?" a waitress slapped down some menus, silverware and napkins.

"Oh, nothing for me," Marcie said. "We're just here for the entertainment."

"You either buy something or you're out of here."

"Oh, okay. What do you have on draft?" Marcie asked.

"Bud and Summer Shandy."

"Do you have any craft beer?" Gwen asked.

The waitress laughed and called over to the bar. "Hey, Joe, the girls want to know if you have any craft beer." The sound of laughter echoed in the almost empty room.

"We'll take two Bud Lights." Marcie pulled out her driver's license and showed it to the waitress.

"And where's yours?"

"I'll have a coke." Gwen said.

"Sorry, thought maybe we would get away with it," Marcie leaned over and said once the waitress left.

"One more month."

"Hey, girls." Bernie slipped into the remaining chair at their table.

"You owe me big time, Bernie Rogers." Marcie squeezed his arm hard.

"I'm sorry, Marcie. I didn't remember it being this bad. Guess I wasn't paying too much attention back then. I'm sure it's nothing like the bars you are used to at college. I'll take you both some place nice when I'm done."

The door opened and a group of bikers entered, followed by a group of people with two men dressed like Johnny Cash and one dressed like Elvis. Most of them appeared to be in their fifties or older, though there were a couple younger bikers in the group. "Oh, I forgot to tell you. They have karaoke every Saturday night. Some of these singers take it very seriously." Bernie started to stand up. "I've got to go, have to make sure my guitar is tuned up."

"Don't leave us here." Marcie grabbed his hand to prevent him from getting up.

"You'll be okay. It's just a short set of songs then we'll be out of here."

"You owe me," Marcie reminded him as he left.

Two of the younger bikers pulled up chairs to their table.

"I'm sorry, but these chairs are taken," Marcie told them.

"I don't see anyone sitting here," the first biker said.

"They had to slip out to take a call," Gwen told him.

"Then we'll get up when they get back," the second added.

Marcie tried to ignore them as the bar owner went over to the mike to introduce Bernie. "I've got a treat for you. Jack's Bar is proud to introduce a hometown boy, visiting from Nashville, Tennessee where he plays with ... What's the name of your band again?"

"Daryl and the Rough Riders," Bernie told him.

"Give a welcome to Bernie Rogers, guitar player for Daryl and the Rough Riders."

The small crowd booed when Bernie came forward.

"What about karaoke? We came here for karaoke."

"We'll have karaoke after Bernie's done," the owner said. "Come on, give the boy a chance."

"Never heard of them or him," someone shouted.

"Let him be. He's Burt's grandson," one of the men from the bar yelled back.

They continued to complain as Bernie spoke into the microphone.

"Thank you everyone," Bernie stated despite all the grumbling. "As Joe mentioned, I'm Burt Nelson's grandson, visiting from Nashville, Tennessee. It's great to be back in Cascade Falls."

"Sing," someone yelled.

"Yeah, get it over with."

"I'm going to start with a song I wrote called 'Hometown Girl,' dedicated to my hometown girl who is here today, Marcie Taylor." He pointed at Marcie who tried to shrink into the corner.

"Hey, you didn't tell us you were with the guitar player," one of the bikers said.

"Yeah, well ..."

"I remember Bernie back when he was in school. Was always in and out of trouble. He was friends with my youngest brother. They had a few good times together." He shouted over at Bernie. "Hey Bernie, remember me? It's Roger."

Bernie had already started his song. He smiled and nodded at Roger but continued singing.

"Any friend of Bernie's is a friend of mine," Roger told her.

"His grandfather's okay, too. He's friends with my gramps. I'm Bud." The biker sitting next to Gwen reached over to shake her hand. At this Marcie started to relax. It seemed she had two new friends.

About halfway through the song she began to feel uncomfortable again, like someone was staring at her. She turned partway to look at the bar. Her eyes met the stare of one of the men standing there. He raised his glass at her and nodded as if he knew her. Marcie turned away, trying to ignore his stare, but every time she glanced in that direction she was met by his glare. She found herself very happy about the company of their two new friends. It was hard to shut out the glaring face and focus on Bernie's playing, but she assured herself she was safe as long as Roger and Bud were at their table.

"So, how did you like my song? You know, the one I wrote for you." Bernie finished his set and sat down with the group.

"It was great, buddy." Roger slapped his shoulder and shook his hand. "Good to see you again. This here's my friend, Bud." Bud stopped talking to Gwen long enough to nod in Bernie's direction. "How long you going to be in town? We should get together."

"We should do that, Roger. How about I buy you a drink, and one for your friend, too?" Bernie motioned to the waitress, indicating another round for the table.

"Thanks, buddy. I told you he was a good guy," Roger said to Bud, who was too busy talking to Gwen to answer.

The waitress brought the beers and another coke for Gwen.

"Here's your coke." Disdain dripped from her lips as she set it down, banging it on the table.

"These men kept us company while you were singing." Marcie pushed her beer to Bernie.

"I see that. My thanks to you, but we better get going."

"Yeah, we've got that thing." Marcie stood up.

"What thing?" Gwen asked.

"You know, that thing." Marcie nodded her head towards the door.

"Oh, yeah, that thing." Gwen began to stand up.

"You don't have to go with them," Bud put his hand on Gwen's. "I'll make sure your friend gets home," he told Marcie.

"No, that's okay. I have to go." Gwen slipped him a napkin with a phone number on it and headed for the door.

"I'll be right back. I have to settle up with the owner," Bernie went back inside leaving them on the steps.

"You didn't actually give him your number, did you?" Marcie asked.

"I gave him a napkin with a number." Marcie started laughing until she felt someone grab her by the wrist. She turned to face the man from the bar.

"Now where do you think you are going, little lady?"

"Let go of me." Marcie tried to pull away. She was surprised at how strong he was for his age. He was medium height, wizened and wrinkled with age, with dyed black hair and a gold tooth.

"You ain't going nowhere 'less I let you. You are mine, my flesh and blood."

"What are you talking about?"

"You go ask your daddy. Tell him you saw Max. See what he says."

"What's going on here?" Bernie came up from behind and put a protective arm around Marcie. Max let go of her wrist and backed off.

"No harm intended," he said as he backed away. "You ask your daddy," he repeated before turning around and climbing into a car.

"What was that about?" Bernie asked.

"I don't know. He was staring at me all through your set. I'm sorry. I didn't hear your first song because of him. He's creepy. Said something about being my flesh and blood and to ask my dad. I don't know what he was talking about. I'm sorry I didn't hear your song."

"Don't worry about that. What's important is that you're okay. I can always do a special encore just for you," Bernie said as he walked them to Gwen's car. "I'm sorry I dragged you two here. I didn't realize how bad it would be. I really wanted to dedicate that song to you and have you hear it."

Gwen stepped forward. "It wasn't so bad and I enjoyed hanging out with Roger and Bud."

"I owe you both dinner. How about I meet you at the diner?"

"Anywhere but here works for me," Marcie said as she climbed into Gwen's car.

Chapter 26

It wasn't late when Bernie dropped her home. Marcie's dad was still up, sitting in his chair reading the paper. Marcie sat down on the couch across from him, wondering how to broach the subject of Max without letting him know where she had gone.

"Dad, how come you never told me anything about Mom?"

"You never asked." Her dad stopped reading and looked at her.

"That's because I knew it would upset you if I asked. I didn't want to lose the only parent I had."

"I'm sorry. I know it upset me, but you could have asked anyway. You know you'd never lose me." He put the paper down. "Where did you go tonight?"

"Jack's Bar, but that's not important." Marcie switched the topic back before he could respond. "Anyway, I'm asking now. What happened? I know you said she died when I was a baby, but how? What was she like?"

"Wasn't I enough? Aren't I enough? And your Aunt Jean. She helped out. Wasn't that enough?"

"You were great, Dad. I always knew you loved me. And Aunt Jean too. But I always wondered about Mom. I always missed Mom."

"How can you miss something you never had?"

Marcie had said the same thing to herself repeatedly over the years. Now she knew where she had gotten it. She shifted forward in her seat and looked directly at her father.

"Because everywhere I looked I was reminded about what I didn't have. Everywhere there were girls with their moms. You tried, Dad. You did your best. But you weren't Mom. Aunt Jean helped, but she wasn't there all the time, just when you called on her. She wasn't Mom."

"I'm sorry, baby. I tried so hard to make it up to you."

"I know. I'm not angry. I just want to know more about Mom. How come there are no pictures of her?"

"I have one. I keep it in my wallet. Here. It was taken when she was pregnant with you. I love this picture. My two best girls." Her dad handed her the picture from his wallet.

"She looks so young."

"She was young. Just sixteen."

"Sixteen? Weren't you married?"

"Yes, I married your mother against my parent's wishes. Did you ever wonder why Grandma and Grandpa didn't come over more often? Weren't more involved in your life?"

"I guess I always thought it was something I did."

"No, it was because of your mom. They didn't approve of her. Never approved of her, but oh, your mom was a beauty. She lit up the room. I loved her from the moment I met her."

"When did you meet?"

Henry paused to give himself time to go back over the years. "Let's see. I was eight, your mom was six."

"So young."

"It seems I knew her all my life, loved her all my life. We grew up together, were together all the time."

"Like me and Bernie until he moved away."

"Kind of. But her dad was mean. He used to beat her mom and then when that wasn't enough, he beat her too. He did other things to her, unspeakable things. I didn't know it back then, only found out later. When your mom turned thirteen, it was as if she went wild, drinking, drugs, men. I tried to talk to her, but she would have nothing to do with me, said I was too good for her. In actuality, she was too good for me. She had been more sinned against than sinning herself. She suffered much in this life."

"But you got together, didn't you?"

"Not right away." Henry paused. "Those were painful years, watching your mother self-destruct."

"I met a man named Max tonight. He said to ask you about him."

"He did? What did he tell you?"

"He said we were flesh and blood. What was he talking about?"

Her dad paused again. Finally the words were dragged from his mouth as if pulling out a distasteful piece of fat or a disgusting hair. "He's your grandfather."

"My grandfather?"

"Yes. I didn't know he was back in town."

"Why didn't you tell me about him before this?"

"Because I never wanted you to meet him or know anything about him. Not after what he did to your mother. I didn't want him anywhere near you. I was protecting you."

"Like you protected my mother?"

"I wanted to protect your mother, but I couldn't. She ran away from home. I couldn't follow her. I was too young, only sixteen at the time. I tried to forget her and I did for a while. Then she came back. As abruptly as she had left, she was back. Only sixteen and pregnant."

"With me?" Marcie sat back in her chair.

"Yes, with you. No one would take her in, not her parents, not her grandparents. Her dad said she had brought judgment upon herself. Would have nothing to do with her. I had just graduated from high school and was preparing to start college. I couldn't abandon her or the child she carried. So, we ran away and were married. I pulled some strings to get into married housing. That way I didn't have to give up my scholarship. I went to school and worked part time. Your mom worked part time too, until you were born. Then she stayed home to take care of you." Henry droned on as if unaware of how his words were being received.

"Those were good days, happy days, but they didn't last. I wasn't enough for your mom. I couldn't heal all those years of abuse, try though I might. She ran away again, left me a note saying I was too good for her and asking me to take care of her daughter. Like I could do anything else, like I could abandon the baby girl she gave to me."

"So, you aren't my father? I'm not your daughter?" Marcie tried to get up, steadying herself as her head swam.

"You were more precious to me than flesh and blood, are more precious. You are my darling baby girl and always will be."

"You aren't my father?" Marcie repeated as she struggled to let the words settle in. She sat back down in her chair. "But what happened to my mom?"

"I never saw her again. At first she sent me notes, always without return addresses to keep me from tracking her down. But the notes became fewer and fewer, always from a new city, another state. One day I received a call from a police officer in Aspen, Colorado. How and why she went there, I don't know. Her body had been found in a snow mound. There was no sign of foul play. She had died of an overdose. Her only possessions had been a backpack. They gave the backpack to me. Inside had been a change of underwear and socks, a few tops, and a baby picture of you. She had died as she had lived, alone."

"I think I remember one winter, you leaving me with Aunt Jean while you went somewhere. I was maybe five."

"Yes. I had gone to Colorado to take care of her one last time."

"I remember you had been very sad."

"I never wanted you to know. I wanted you to have your image of a mother who loved you, not a tortured soul who abandoned you and her husband and died in a snow mound."

"Then why are you telling me now?"

"Because you asked and because of your grandfather. He had threatened to tell you before, back when you were still little. I paid him off back then, told him to get out of town and never return. That was the bargain. I paid for his silence and leaving you alone. He must be back for more money. He's letting me know that he knows who you are."

"This is too much. Too much to take in at one time."

"I was protecting you."

"My mother didn't just die, she abandoned me. And the man I knew to be my father, isn't really my father. I can't breathe. I have to leave." Marcie stood up.

"Legally, socially, emotionally, in every way but biologically, I am your father. Isn't that enough?" Her dad stood up as well and reached out to stop her.

"I don't know. I don't know what to think. Do you know who my father is?" Marcie steadied herself by holding onto a chair. "It's not, that man, my grandfather, is it?"

"No, your mother made sure of that by running away from home. She never talked about your father. I'm not sure she knew. You just don't realize how badly she had been hurt, how damaged by her father's abuse. If only you had known her as I knew her."

"But I don't. I don't know anything about her. And now, I wonder what I know about you." Marcie started towards the door.

"You understand why I couldn't say anything before this. I wouldn't have said anything if he hadn't shown up, if I had thought I could have continued to keep it secret. I would have carried it to my grave. Your mother did love you, with all her heart. She believed you were better off without her, better off in my care. That's why she came back to Cascade Falls. That's why she married me. Not because she loved me, but because she wanted a father for her daughter."

"Too much, Dad. Too much. I have to get out of here." Marcie ran out of the room, down the steps of the back porch, hopped on her bicycle and rode.

Chapter 27

Where should I go? Who can I turn to? I can't go home. Her mind was racing faster than her bike. She rode to the park and considered running away, but where? And how? She had left without any identification, any money. She wouldn't be able to get far. Apparently she was far less resourceful than her mother had been. There was only one place she could go. She drove to Bernie's grandparents' home and knocked on the door.

"What are you doing here, Marcie? What's wrong?" Bernie asked when he answered the door. "Why didn't you call? You're shaking." He steadied her with his arm and walked her down the steps. They sat down on the front step, his arm still around her.

"I didn't know where to go. I can't go home."

"But, but why? What's wrong?"

"I just can't. I can't explain right now. Can I stay with you?"

"Marcie, this is my grandparents' home."

"I know, but I don't know where else to go."

"What do I tell my grandparents?"

"Don't tell them anything. Can't you sneak me in?"

Marcie heard the back door open.

"Bernie, who's there?" Bernie's grandma walked out onto the porch. Marcie ducked behind a bush, looked at him and silently pleaded with him.

"No one, Grandma. I just stepped out for some fresh air."

"Don't be silly, child. I heard someone knock. Is that Marcie?"

"Yes, Grandma."

"Well come out, child. Bring the girl in out of the damp."

"Okay, Grandma." Marcie slowly came out of the bushes. Bernie took her hand, gave her a look of reassurance, and encouraged her to walk up the stairs.

"I'm so sorry to bother you. I just didn't know where else to go," Marcie said as she walked through the door.

"You did the right thing, child. We are always happy to have one of Bernie's friends over. We were expecting you."

"You were?" Marcie had welcomed the warm hug from Bernie's grandmother but pulled back at this.

"Yes, your father called. Said he thought you were headed this way."

"What else did he tell you?"

"Enough. Enough to know you need a warm hug and a cup of cocoa."

"No, thank you. I don't want you to bother."

"No bother. Sit down. A cup of cocoa never hurt anyone and just might do some good." Marcie looked over at Bernie before sitting down at the kitchen table.

"You sit down too." She directed Bernie who quietly sat down next to Marcie.

"Your dad said you were asking about your mother. I always thought this day would come. I had promised your dad not to say anything, but now, well, now I guess it's time."

"You knew my mother?"

"There are no secrets in this town."

"That's funny because this is one I never knew."

"That's because your daddy never wanted you to know. It was for your own good. Those that knew kept silent out of respect for your dad. But I remember your mother and your father, back when they were young."

"He's not my father."

"Whatever nonsense have you been listening to? He's your father and a good one at that. You should be proud to call Henry Taylor your father." Alvina placed a cup of cocoa in front of Marcie and sat down across from her. "Your mom was wild. She had a self-destructive streak, but she loved your dad and he loved her, and she loved you enough to give you to him. Isn't that enough?"

"It's not enough. My whole world, what I thought to be true, it's all lies. How can I believe anything anymore?"

"Believe this," Alvina took Marcie's hands between her own and locked her gaze into Marcie's eyes. "Your father loves you more than life itself. Why else would he sacrifice all he did, putting off college when your mom left, then working so hard to raise you while going to school, saving every penny to provide you with a home and food and a good life. That, my child, is love. Love, solid and true, not love made up in dreams. That is something you can believe in."

Marcie wanted to believe. This wasn't a leap of faith requiring belief in something you can't see. This was belief based on something she had witnessed all of her life, belief in a father who loved her. How could she not believe?

"I guess I know that. But I still can't go home tonight. Can I stay here?"

"Of course you can. Your dad thought that might be the case. You can sleep in Bernie's room." She looked at Bernie. "You, young man, will be sleeping on the sofa. It's all decided. Drink up your cocoa." Alvina sat with them as Marcie slowly sipped the cocoa.

"Does everybody know?" Marcie asked.

"Not everybody, but it was hard to hide a pregnant teen and a quick marriage. Your dad took your mom away to get married, then he took her off to college with him so it wasn't such a big deal when she showed up pregnant during Christmas break and later showed up with a baby. I knew more than most because I had been friends with your grandma."

"Grandma Taylor?"

"No, your mom's mother."

"You knew my grandma." Marcie stopped sipping the hot cocoa and looked up. "Is she still alive? I never knew her, never met her."

"I'm sorry, child. Your grandma died years ago. It about broke her heart, what happened to your mom. When you were born, she wanted to come see you, wanted desperately to see you and your mother. But her husband ..." Alvina shook her head as she spoke. "I won't dignify him with the term grandfather, just as he never deserved the name father after how he treated his girl, and his wife, too. Anyway, her husband forbid it and she wasn't about to go against her husband. She had bruises and broken bones from him for the least infraction, whether real or made up by him. All she had to do was look at him and he would take it wrong and beat her. But she was happy to know you were being taken care of, that her daughter had at least found a good man to raise her granddaughter." Bernie's grandmother reached over and took Marcie's hands in hers.

"When the news came that Emily was dead, that was what killed her. She couldn't take it. It took the heart out of her. She never had the will to stand up to her husband, so beaten down she was. But she just stopped caring. Stopped taking care of her clothes. Stopped ironing his shirts, cooking his meals. The funny thing was, once she stopped caring, he stopped beating on her. Ain't seen nothing like it before. He even started taking care of her. But it was no good. She wasted away. Stopped eating, stopped everything."

"What about my grand ... her husband?"

"He moved away. I suspect he found someone else to beat on. I helped with the laying out, picked out clothes for your grandma to wear. I know it's unchristian, but I have no kind words to say about her husband, even though he seemed to have changed at the end. I didn't believe it though. Men like that, they don't change. Some people don't deserve forgiveness. After what he did to your mother ... I hope he rots in hell."

"Grandma," Bernie's voice broke into her narrative.

"Well, I do. You're grown up now. You can deal with such things, not like when you were little. Then I had to protect you, just as your dad protected you." Alvina looked back at Marcie.

"Was that the man at the bar?" Bernie asked.

"I heard he was back in town. Up to no good I suspect," Alvina said.

"He grabbed me by the wrist, said I was his," Marcie said.

"He knew that your father wasn't the biological father. It wasn't that hard to figure out if you did the math. You had been born after they had only been married five months. Most that gave it any thought, figured that was why they got married. Your dad, being the honorable man that he was, would never have abandoned your mom after getting her pregnant. As far as anyone knew, he had been seeing her before they got married. I knew differently, and so did your grandma's husband. I suspect he had been using this to get money out of your dad. He had come back into town a few years after his wife's death. You were eight or nine then. He saw you, talked to you."

"I thought he looked vaguely familiar. There had been this one man, watching me on the playground at school. He'd been creepy. He had talked to me, said he had something for me. I ran away from him, like I had been taught, and told my teacher. He wasn't around after that."

"He had talked to your dad at work. I saw it because at that time I had been a secretary at your dad's law firm. I recognized him, knew he was up to no good. I remember it like it was yesterday. He came over to me and leered at me. 'Alvina, you are looking good,' he'd said. It was all I could do to keep from hitting him on the head with a paper weight. He grinned, that awful, greasy grin he had and I haven't seen him since. Rumor was that your dad gave him money to stay away from you. And now he's back, up to no good."

"That's why dad told me his secret."

"Better that it come from him than from that man. Your dad would have kept it to his grave. All I can say is that he better not be coming near me or anyone I love. I'll take my frying pan to him."

"Grandma, I never saw this side of you before," Bernie said.

"There's lots you don't know about me, young man. Some men don't deserve forgiveness."

"What about my mom, Grandma? Is there forgiveness for her?" Bernie asked.

"No matter what your mama does, she is still my daughter. I can't condemn her. I may condemn her actions. I know I don't approve of them, but I don't condemn her. She did one thing right."

"What was that, Grandma?"

"She gave me a precious grandson, three precious grandsons to be precise."

"What are you yammering about old woman?" Bernie's grandfather came in from the front room where he had been sleeping in front of the TV. "Look at what time it is."

"None of your business, old man. And I'm aware of the time. It's time to get these young folk to bed."

Chapter 28

Marcie turned over in the bed that smelt of Bernie. Wrapped in the smell, she felt safe and secure and slept soundly. In the early morning fog between sleep and wake, she thought she heard someone breathing next to her. Could it be? No, stretched out on the bed was Bernie's dog, Blade. She reached over and scratched the dog's ears. Blade turned over on his back and moaned in dog pleasure.

But then she remembered why she was here, the events of the previous night. Surely it had just been a bad dream, she told herself. Then she saw the tight jeans and skimpy top she had worn last night. She didn't want to put them on. They reeked of shame.

She had worn one of Bernie's t-shirts to bed. Lying next to the bed was a bathrobe provided by Bernie's grandma, cotton cloth with flower print. Not something she would have picked for herself, but better than putting on those clothes. She wrapped the bathrobe around her and tied it at the waist as she heard a gentle rap on her door.

"You up?" Bernie's voice came through the door.

"Yes."

He cracked the door open slightly. "You dressed?"

"Yes, sort of."

"Dang," he feigned disappointment. Bernie walked in and looked her over. "Grandma's bathrobe never looked better."

"Ha ha. I'm sure I'm a sight." Marcie tugged at the cotton material.

"You could say that." He kissed her before adding, "Coffee's ready. Come on down and have some. And Grandma's got eggs and bacon frying."

"I'm not hungry."

"You know Grandma. She'll never accept that as an answer."

"All right. I'll be down in a minute."

"Come on, Blade, you dumb dog. Get off that bed." Blade slowly rolled out of bed and followed Bernie down the stairs.

Bernie's grandparents were in their church clothes when Marcie joined them at the kitchen table.

"Sit down, honey, and have some coffee," Alvina insisted. As Marcie sat down she brought over a plate of scrambled eggs and bacon. "There's toast on the plate over there, help yourself."

"I'm not that hungry," Marcie stated.

"Nonsense. A young girl like you needs her strength." She put the plate in front of her. "Now eat up."

"Leave the girl be," Burt told her. "Give her a minute to taste her coffee." Alvina ignored him as she cleared Burt's and her dishes.

"I'll take care of these, Grandma." Bernie took the plates away from her.

"I guess we better be going to church." She looked at Bernie as he put the plates in the sink. "Make sure you run some water on them."

"I know, Grandma, so the eggs don't stick to the plate." He turned on the faucet.

"I take it you're not coming with us."

"No," Bernie was dressed in jeans and a white t-shirt. "Why should today be different than any other Sunday?"

Alvina looked at Marcie. "There best be no hanky-panky while we're gone."

"Let the boy be." Burt got up from the table and winked at his grandson. "I'm sure he can take care of the situation. We best be on our way."

"I probably should be on my way too," Marcie said.

"No, stay. Finish your breakfast. Don't mind her," Burt said before leaving.

"I really should be getting home. I don't have any clean clothes here." Marcie looked down at the bathrobe.

"Are you sure you are ready to go home?" Bernie asked.

"I guess I'm as ready as I'll ever be. Where else can I go?"

"You can stay here. I don't mind the couch. We can get your things while your dad's at church. You won't have to talk to him at all."

"No, that's okay. Home is where I belong." Marcie took a bite of scrambled eggs and realized she was hungry after all. She finished the eggs and bacon with a piece of toast while Bernie watched and grinned.

"I guess last night didn't affect your appetite any."

"I guess not." She slid the plate aside and took a sip of coffee, breathing in the aroma. "You know, I guess it was for the best, finding out about my mom and all. I think there was a part of me always knew something wasn't right about the story Dad had told me. I knew something was wrong, I just didn't know what." Marcie stared off in space, lost in thought.

"I think maybe I knew more than I realized. I knew there was something about my mother." Marcie took another sip as she thought out loud. "I remember a girl at school called my mother a name. I didn't know what it meant, I just knew whatever it was, it wasn't good. In fact, from the way she said it, I knew it was something awful."

Bernie put his hand over hers.

"I think that was when Dad put me in the Lutheran school. He said he talked to the pastor and it was all set. No one knew my mother there, but everyone knew and respected my dad. And if they did know something, I think Dad thought they might be less cruel." Marcie took a sip of coffee. "How did you end up at St. Luke's?"

"My grandma thought it would be good for me, that maybe I wouldn't get into as much trouble there as in the public high school. Little did either of them know. She also figured I needed some religion. A lot of good it did either of us. Here we are, sitting at home on a Sunday morning."

Marcie reached over and kissed him. "It did some good. We got to be together while there."

"Hmmmm, hanky-panky," Bernie mumbled through the kiss. "Hmmmm, bacon." He laughed as their lips separated.

"Time for me to get dressed and get home so I can shower and put on clean clothes." Marcie stood up.

"Need any help with that?"

"I think I can manage," she started for the door, then stopped. "It's not good, what I found out, but at least now I know the worst. Nothing worse can happen, can it?"

Chapter 29

Henry was relieved to see Marcie's bike parked in its usual spot by the back steps when he got home. He had asked Burt and Alvina about her when he saw them at church.

"That girl, she's a good one. She'll come around," Alvina had reassured him, and now he knew it was true.

"Marcie?" he called up the stairs.

"Yeah, Dad," she started down the stairs, her hair still wet from her shower.

"You want some breakfast?"

"I ate at Bernie's."

"I brought cinnamon rolls." Cinnamon rolls after church had been their ritual when she had been little. If she behaved in church, he stopped and bought her a cinnamon roll on the way home. It was a bribe, one that worked, one that kept her going to church with him without a lot of fuss and complaining until she went away to college and stopped attending.

"But I didn't go to church."

"We'll let it slide this time."

"Maybe I could eat a bite." She sat at the table and watched him pour water into the coffee brewer, listen for the first perk of coffee, then put the rolls on a plate and set them on the table. Soon the aroma was filling the kitchen.

"So how was church?"

"Church was church. I ran into Bernie's grandparents there."

"Oh," Marcie reached for a roll. Henry stopped her.

"Not till the coffee's ready. You know that."

"But I already had some coffee."

"The rolls are best with a fresh cup of coffee." Marcie left the roll on the plate.

"You know, Marcie, about last night ..."

"I know, Dad. I don't want to talk about it. Okay?"

"That's okay. But if you ever want to talk, you know you can."

"I know." Henry poured two cups of coffee and placed one in front of Marcie as she took a cinnamon roll off the plate. She pulled it apart, relishing its sugary richness.

"One thing, though Marcie, that you need to be aware of." Her dad sat down.

"Oh?" Marcie stopped the bite she was about to take.

"That man, Max, your grandfather, he can't be trusted. I don't know what he's up to, but it may include you. Promise me, whatever he says or does, you won't go near him."

"That's an easy promise to make, Dad. I hope I never see that man again."

"That's my girl." Henry took a gulp of coffee before starting on his cinnamon roll.

The piece of roll Marcie had torn off, continued its journey into her mouth. It didn't taste as good as it usually did.

Chapter 30

Modern Day Slavery

Slavery has been around since Biblical times and it is still present today under a new name, human trafficking. In fact, it has become more popular among many lowlifes today than drug trafficking. Drugs, once you sell them, they are gone, used by the buyer. Humans you can sell over and over again, getting a much better return. The girl trafficked into prostitution provides a steady income with minimal expense and upkeep. She can be sold to multiple buyers, who return her, somewhat worse for wear, but she is returned and able to be sold again.

But prostitution isn't the only venue for human trafficking, just the most well-known. Farm laborers may be kept like prisoners on farms with meager wages that go back to the owner to pay for "housing", such as it is, and food, what little they can afford. The fear of deportation keeps them working under worse conditions than they would experience in a jail setting. The lack of the ability to communicate in English keeps them from getting the help available to them, and threats and misinformation keep them afraid to leave, holding onto the hope of someday being paid the wages owed them.

And then there are house servants, children brought over from their native country to serve rich families as maids, cooks, nannies, all at the same time. They are trapped, kept in ignorance and not allowed contact with anyone outside of the immediate family circle.

Even your local hairdresser can be a home for slaves who work cutting, curling, braiding hair all day and sleep on the floor of rooms above the hair salon. Such was the case for one salon in New York City.

Marcie paused as she wrote this. The image of Mei-Lin popped into her head. Could that be the case? Or was she wrong like so many other times? She pushed the idea away.

Many say these things happen in places like New York City, not small cities like Cascade Falls. But is that so far-fetched? Isn't it possible that the streets of Cascade Falls and the area around the city, especially the I-94 corridor, could hold secrets, dark secrets.

SS

"What's the word at the Dance Studio about Marcie's blog?" Joe asked Kathleen over dinner.

"It's not as popular any more, not since she stopped writing about local gossip. You know teenagers. They are on to the next titillating topic. Nothing holds their interest for too long."

"That's good."

"Is it? I thought it was fun."

"It was?"

"Sure, being the target of a local gossip columnist. Kind of like being a celebrity, written about in those awful tabloids, but on a much smaller scale. Maybe that was our fifteen minutes of fame and we missed it."

"That kind of fame I can do without." Joe stabbed the piece of pork on his plate. Kathleen's turn to cook. "Where is everybody?"

"Scott is out with friends, Mom and Peter have gone out for the night and Grandpa is in his room watching the game. He said he wasn't hungry. Imagine that. You have me all to yourself."

"Oh," Joe said.

"Don't be so enthusiastic."

"Sorry, that's great." Joe feigned enthusiasm as he sawed at his pork chop.

"I thought so," Kathleen said as she chewed on her piece of pork.

They didn't always eat at Kathleen's even on her days to cook. There were too many family members coming and going. At Joe's there was only Michelle who, befitting her status as a new graduate and imminent college student, was rarely home evenings. Stephanie had not come home this summer, choosing to take summer classes and work at the job she had acquired in the city where her college was located. Josh had done the same thing. Kathleen only saw him on those rare occasions when he didn't have classes and didn't have to work. Between his scholarships, grants, loans and his job, he was managing to put himself through college – so who was she to complain? At least he hadn't dropped out like that Marcie character. Josh and Stephanie were attending different colleges in the same city, so when he came home, Stephanie usually hitched a ride with him.

"Any word from Stephanie?" Kathleen asked.

"No, guess I won't hear anything until the next time Josh comes home. Any word from him?" Joe cut off a piece of pork then chewed and chewed to enable it to go down his throat.

"No." Kathleen ignored how he sawed away at the food she had prepared. "I think Marcie just might be onto something."

"About what?"

"About the nail salon." Marcie had shared her suspicions about the nail salon with Joe who had told Kathleen. "All of the teens at the Dance Studio go there. They love it. It's the cheapest place in town to have your nails done. How can they afford to be so cheap?"

"Do you think they have something going on the side?"

"That thought did cross my mind, but no, I don't think so. Not enough male clientele. I went there myself to check it out. See?" Kathleen showed him her newly polished nails.

"Nice."

"And so cheap." She pulled her hands back. "Something's not right."

"You attend one trafficking awareness workshop with me and suddenly you're an expert."

"Not on human trafficking, but I do know something about criminal activity."

"The problem is that if they are here illegally, they will be deported. Who knows what kind of situation you may be sending them back to? We have to be careful, do our homework before rushing in."

"If these girls aren't being held against their will, they are at least being abused, not just by the owner, but by her son as well. The youngest looks like she could be maybe sixteen, if that old."

"I'll see what I can find out. Get with some of my contacts through the Anti-Trafficking Network and the police force."

"No, we'll see what we can find out. You aren't leaving me out of this."

Joe pushed his unfinished plate away. "Dinner was delicious. I just don't seem to have much of an appetite tonight."

"I'll pack you a doggie bag so you can have it for lunch tomorrow." Kathleen cleared his plate and came back with a brown bag with a grease stain on the side. "Here you are."

Chapter 31

Henry wasn't surprised when Max showed up unannounced at his law office.

"There's a man here to see you. Says you are expecting him. His name is Max."

"That's okay, Delores, send him in." Yes, he had been expecting him, if not today, then someday. Men like Max don't just go away. Henry remained seated behind his desk as Max entered. He didn't stand up to greet him, didn't shake his hand. Undismayed by this, Max sat down in the seat across from Henry.

"You're wasting your time, Max. Marcie already knows about you. I told her this weekend. So you might as well go back to wherever you came from. You're not getting any more money from me."

"You're thinking all I care about is money. I have a granddaughter doesn't even know me. Me being her own flesh and blood, which is more than you can say." The gold tooth glittered from under his lip.

"What are you getting at?"

"I just might want to stick around, get to know my granddaughter. It seems to me a crying shame that she doesn't know me. She being all the kin I have left."

"You stay away from her."

"How high a value do you place on your daughter?"

"I paid you once. You were never to come back."

"But that was over ten years ago. A man has needs. He gets older and he starts thinking about family."

"How much would it take for you to go away and never come back?"

"I'm thinking one hundred thousand dollars would be a nice sum. You got a nice fancy office here." Max looked around the office. "Must be doing quite well for yourself."

"That's twice what I paid you last time."

"And I was a fool to accept it. Consider it back pay."

"How do I know you won't come back again?"

"You got my word. I'll swear on my granddaughter's life. One hundred thousand and I'll be gone. You'll never see me again."

"And if not?"

"As I said, I just might move back to Cascade Falls so I can be close to my granddaughter. You wouldn't deny a man that, would you? That's worth an awful lot of money. Will take a lot to make up for not seeing her."

"I have to think about it. That's a lot of money. It will take me a while to get it." Henry put him off.

"Don't take too long. Who knows how much time I have left. And that granddaughter of mine, she is one sweet girl, if you know what I mean."

"Get out of my office." Henry stood up. "I'll be in touch."

"That you will." Max sauntered out the door, leaving it open on his way out. He stopped at Delores' desk. "You know, I could use a sweet thing like you to show me around the town."

Henry came into the reception room.

"Max was just leaving, weren't you, Max?" Max nodded at Delores as he left.

"Who was that?" Delores asked.

"No one you need to be concerned with. Get me Andy on the phone."

Chapter 32

The Case of the Hello Kitty bike

Today we'll be exploring the mystery of the Hello Kitty bike. While riding my bike the other day to Otter Lake, I came across someone sleeping in one of those zippered hammocks, you know the kind that zips shut to keep bugs out and prying eyes away. Next to the hammock was a backpack with a box of brown sugar cinnamon Pop-tarts, Vitamin Water and Mountain Dew. And beside that was a Hello Kitty bike, black with a pink seat and handle bars.

Who might this sleeping beauty be? Some escapee from a juvie home? Maybe a runaway? Does the bike belong to the sleeper, or was it stolen from a back yard or front lawn? If anyone has clues to solve this mystery, let me know. Comment below or email me at info@delicioussecrets.com

And what about the dangling tennis shoes? Could the two be connected?

SS

"You doing okay? You're awfully quiet today." Bernie reached over and put his hand under her chin, forcing her to look up at him as they shared burgers at the Burger Barn.

"No, yeah, or I'm okay. It's just ever since I met that 'man' I just get the feeling that he's watching me."

"Have you seen him?"

"No, just a feeling, probably nothing, but my dad seemed to think we weren't done with him yet." Marcie swallowed her last bite of burger. Bernie reached over wiped ketchup from where it had lingered on her mouth.

"If he tries anything ... You know, I'm pretty good with a gun."

"No, and that's something I'd rather not know."

"I'm just saying, you can count on me."

"He hasn't tried anything and probably won't. Nothing for you to worry about. Besides, I have other concerns to occupy my mind." She picked up a French fry and held it in mid-air as she thought.

"I'm hoping I'm one of them." Bernie squeezed her hand as he said this.

"You are concerning, and disconcerting, but no, my world doesn't revolve around you." Marcie ignored the pressure on her hand.

"I'm not sure I like that."

"You know I've been doing research on human trafficking?"

"Yes, but what has that to do with me?"

"I keep wondering about that nail salon. Something's not right. Gwen tells me to leave it alone. We've got a good thing. She doesn't want me to mess it up, but I can't let it go." She pushed the remaining French fries over to Bernie.

"Have you talked to Pastor about it?" Bernie ate the French fries four at a time.

"Yeah, but I've been wrong too many times. He told me I needed evidence, not just suspicions."

"So how do we get this evidence?"

"I was hoping you would say that. I've been thinking, maybe I should case the joint, you know a stake-out, only it's hard to do this on a bike, and I work from nine to three every week day. That's where you come in."

"I'm listening." Bernie finished off what was left of the French fries in one swallow.

"You could park your truck within view of the salon, watch who comes and goes."

"Don't you think my truck would be conspicuous?"

"Don't always park in the same spot. And you don't have to stay all day. There's a lunch place across the street from the salon, and a twenty-four-hour laundromat. You could get lunch. And then do some laundry."

"That's a lot of laundry."

"Well, what do you suggest?"

"Let's think about this. Watching who comes and goes during the day isn't going to get us anywhere. All we'll see are the regular customers. It's not like they are smuggling drugs or moving more girls through the place. What we need to see is what the girls do after work. Do they go anywhere? Where does the boss lady go at night? Maybe, if we could just check out the upstairs where you say the girls stay."

"What are you suggesting?"

"You got any laundry? We can go to the laundromat tonight, after the shop closes, watch for any suspicious activity." Marcie jumped up.

"Where are you going?" Bernie asked as she cleared away the remains of their meal and picked up the tray.

"To get some laundry."

Three hours of laundry later and they had seen nothing. Marcie had brought a pile of heavy towels, thinking they would take the longest to dry. She and Bernie sat facing the window, looking across the street into the store. They could see a light in a room above the store and at times a shadow of movement, but nothing suspicious yet.

"What did you expect to see?" Bernie asked. "We already know the girls live upstairs. That's no mystery. How about I get us something to eat?"

"Sure," Marcie dismissed him. She thought she saw the curtain moving just enough to see into the room. It would be too obvious to use binoculars in the bright glare of the laundry room. She would have to go outside, find some dark space where she could watch unobserved. "Don't be gone too long."

She walked down the street to an alleyway where she could hide in the shadows. She pulled up the binoculars, nothing. She could see into the rooms but just barely. She thought she saw one of the girls, but not Mei-Lin. She decided to cross the street and check out the dumpster behind their building. She flashed the pocket light she had brought with her into the dumpster. She didn't know what she was looking for, just that that was what they did on all the crime shows she watched on TV.

The dumpster was full of pretty much what you would expect from a nail salon. Empty polish bottles, used tissues and cotton balls. There was also food waste, fast food bags. That only told her that the workers had been eating. Again, nothing suspicious or incriminating.

"Did you find what you were looking for?" The light glinted off a gold tooth. Marcie recognized the man from the bar, Max.

"Matter of fact, I did. Now I better be going. My boyfriend is supposed to be meeting me any time now."

"Not so fast, little girl. You ain't going anywhere." He grabbed her by the wrist, but this time Marcie was ready for him. She kneed him in the groin, hit him with her backpack and ran. Marcie looked up and down the street, watching for Bernie's truck. She saw it as she heard groans coming from the alley. She ran to the truck and jumped in.

"We've got to go."

"What about the laundry?"

"Leave it. We have to get out of here. We can come back later."

Bernie took off down the street. "Tell me what this is about."

"Max. He tried to grab me. He must have been following us."

"He tried to grab you in the laundromat?"

"No, in the alley behind the nail salon."

"What were you doing there? Wait, don't tell me, you were going through the dumpster." Even in the dark, Marcie could see the displeasure on Bernie's face. "Why didn't you wait for me?"

"Because I didn't think you would let me."

"So instead you risk your life, and for what? Did you find anything?"

"Well, no ..."

"Marcie, this is real life, not TV. You've got to stop acting like you are living in a TV movie. You are not a detective, leave the detective work for the police."

"But Max was real."

"Leave Max to me."

By the time they came back to the laundromat, someone had taken all their towels, leaving behind a small mound of socks and underwear.

"How are we going to explain this to your dad?" Bernie asked.

"We'll think of something," Marcie assured him as they pulled into the driveway

"Marcie, what do you think you were doing? What did you expect to find?" Her dad had been as angry as Marcie had expected, but not about the towels as much as he was angry about her getting into a position where she could have been hurt. "I can buy new towels. I can't buy a new you. And you," he turned and faced Bernie, "how could you have left her alone like that?"

"Someone had to stay with the laundry." Bernie's voice took on a sheepish tone before Henry's anger.

"And what did you think you would find in the alley?" Henry turned to Marcie.

"Dad, don't you think it's suspicious that these Vietnamese girls at the nail salon never go anywhere else? They work there, live there. Doesn't that sound funny to you?"

"Maybe they are undocumented. Maybe that's why they don't go anywhere, out of fear of being deported."

"But, don't you see, Dad? That's how traffickers work. They keep them afraid of the police or anyone who could help them out of fear of deportation. Don't they have to have green cards in order to work in the salon?"

"They are supposed to have them, that doesn't mean they do."

"Cascade Falls is not Chicago or Detroit. There aren't that many immigrants here. Don't you think the police would notice?" Marcie continued her line of inquiry.

"Not unless you bring it to their attention. Do you really want to do that?" Her dad asked.

"I don't know." Marcie slowed down.

"I'm telling you, Marcie, even if they are being trafficked, it can be a long process for them to get the authorization to stay in the country. You don't know what you are dealing with. I think its best that you leave it alone." Marcie sat down. She felt defeated. Her dad's voice softened. "And as for Max, leave him to me. I'm working on him. I'll get a personal protection order against him tomorrow. It won't necessarily keep him away, but at least it will put him on notice and it will alert the police about this character."

Chapter 33

"You know, whenever Bernie's around, it's as if I don't exist." Gwen stated. Marcie looked at her best friend. Was she feeling neglected?

"That's not true."

"Yes, it is. You're always with him. Only time I get to spend with you is when he's busy."

"But he's only going to be here for a short time."

"You didn't have time for me in high school either until he left."

Perhaps Gwen was right about her neglecting her when Bernie was around, Marcie thought. It seemed that Bernie and Gwen had always been a part of her life, each filling in for the other. About the time during high school when Gwen's mom had gotten worse, Bernie had come back into her life, with his own set of secrets. But that didn't mean she valued Gwen any less. They both were essential to her being. Both held secrets Marcie didn't know, as well as the secrets they had shared, kept between the two of them. Just as Marcie had learned to not press Bernie about his family or where he had gone years ago, she didn't press Gwen to tell her about her mom.

"Okay, let's plan some fun. Just you and me."

"What theme?"

"Why Southern ladies, of course," Marcie stated.

"So, where should we go? The college theater department is putting on Shakespeare in the park. Want to check it out? I think they are doing Midsummer Night's Dream."

"Sounds fun. Bernie never wants to go to anything like that."

They agreed to get dressed up in long skirts, sleeveless summer tops and floppy hats and go to the Crab Shack for mocktails and sandwiches. They lounged on the patio, sipping their drinks, enjoying the view and laughing. Afterwards they drove to the park and strolled over to the crowd that had gathered for the play. They stood on the outskirts of the crowd that had already taken up the seats on the few makeshift bleachers that had been put up.

"I guess we should have planned ahead and brought some folding chairs," Gwen said as Marcie slipped off her sandals and let her toes wiggle in the grass.

"That's okay. We can stand. It's better for us." Marcie was soon caught up in the Elizabethan dialogue.

"Too bad we don't have any Elizabethan clothes," Gwen whispered in her ear. "I should have checked out the theater department costumes."

Marcie laughed. "They would have been too hot," she said. Then, distracted from the play, she thought she saw someone on the other side of the bleachers looking at her. When she stared back, whoever it was, was gone.

"Something wrong?" Gwen asked as she followed Marcie's gaze.

"Nothing. I thought I saw something, someone."

"Not that creepy Max?"

"No, it was nothing." Still, Marcie moved away from the crowd to be able to see the other side of the park. She thought she saw a pair of legs disappearing into the trees, but then they were gone. She shivered despite the warmth of the summer sun.

"You cold?"

"I'm fine," Marcie assured her. Marcie struggled to focus on the rest of the play, failing to get caught up in the words as she kept feeling like she was being watched. She was relieved when Gwen's phone rang.

"What's wrong?" Marcie asked when Gwen completed the call.

"That was my dad. Mom's in the hospital. I have to go."

"I'll go with you," Marcie insisted as they climbed into Gwen's car. Gwen didn't fight Marcie on this as she drove to the hospital.

They went into the emergency room and were instructed to wait.

"She'd been okay. She'd been doing so much better. She told me to go out with my friends. I should have known something was up," Gwen rambled while Marcie listened. Gwen's dad came out of the ER with another doctor and led them to a private room.

"She's all right," Gwen's dad said. Marcie tagged along, trying to slip into the room unnoticed lest she be sent out.

"I'm sorry, Dad. I thought she was okay," Gwen began apologizing to her father. "She told me she was okay."

Marcie felt the unspoken words between father and daughter as they exchanged looks, enfolding Gwen in guilt. Marcie sat down next to Gwen and wrapped her arm around her friend's shoulder.

"It's not uncommon for this to happen," the other doctor began. "When in a depressive state, a person doesn't have enough energy to hurt themselves. Sometimes, it's when the depression starts to lift that they tell themselves they can't live through another such episode and try to take their life. But she's okay. We got her here in time. She'll need to spend some time here before she comes home."

"Can I see her now?" Gwen asked.

"I don't think that's advisable." The doctor looked over at Gwen's dad, then at Marcie. "Is there someone to stay with you?"

"I can stay with her, Dr. Thompson," Marcie told Gwen's dad. Marcie went home with Gwen. When Gwen couldn't sleep they sat up on the couch watching videos until Dr. Thompson got home.

"Mom still doing okay?" Gwen asked.

"Yes, why aren't you in bed?"

"We couldn't sleep."

Dr. Thompson sighed, looked at the two young women huddled together on the couch. "Don't stay up too late," he said before going upstairs.

"You know," Gwen said after he left, "Sometimes I wish that she wasn't okay."

"What do you mean?"

"I know it's terrible, but sometimes I wish she would put an end to it, not just for herself, but for all of us. She's miserable and she makes all of us miserable. Have you ever wondered why my brothers and sister never come home?"

"I guess I haven't given it much thought."

"Well, think about it. It's because of her. They've finally gotten away from her while I'm still trapped here."

"You don't mean that."

"And it's because of him, too. Someday I'm going to get away from here myself and when I do, I'm never coming back." Marcie sat in silence with her friend.

Chapter 34

Impending Doom and Global Warming

    We've had a relatively cool summer. Some hot days, but not overly so. Everybody says, "What about global warming?" We think and believe based on our own particular space in time, our experience and our own personal comfort zone and bias. But does that make it true?

    In the 1960s there was a book, Silent Spring, written by a woman named Rachel Carson. It predicted a time when there would be no more songbirds because of pesticides. That didn't come to pass because action was taken to prevent it. Now we are looking at the honey bee population declining at an alarming rate. Honey bees are necessary to cross pollinate plants. Without them crops will fail creating food shortages.

    Sometimes you have to get out of your comfort zone. Just because you aren't affected by the weather events in other parts of the country and world, doesn't mean you will be immune forever. By the time the effects of global warming hit us, it may be too late, may already be too late to stop what scientists throughout the world are predicting.

    Where is the book to move our society to action? To keep us from a flowerless spring because of the lack of honey bees? To save us from flooded coastal areas and torrential storms?

    Who will write this book? Who will read it once written? And who will listen?

                                        SS

Ashley was riding through the park after helping Marcie with the bulletin, when she heard the sound of guitars twanging. She followed the sound to a secluded area where two boys who appeared to be about her age were strumming guitars to the beat of a girl drummer, hitting a practice pad. Ashley recognized the drummer from school but not the boys. She rode closer.

"What are you doing?" she asked.

"What does it look like we are doing?" the first guitar player stated, grumbling as he tuned his guitar.

"Hi, Ashley," the girl smiled at her. "It's Kara, from school."

"Oh, yeah. Hi," Ashley lied. It seems Kara had been as insignificant in her mind as she had been to Janene and company.

"Hi," the other guitarist grinned. "I'm Jesse."

"Enough small talk. Are we going to talk or play guitars?" the first guitar player said.

"And that's Caleb," Jesse said.

"From what I heard, you are better off talking," Ashley said.

"What do you know about music?" Caleb asked.

"I know enough to know what's good and what isn't. Yours isn't."

"You think you're so smart. Let's see you play something," Caleb issued a challenge.

"Happy to." Ashley got off her bike and took Caleb's guitar. She strummed a few chords, made adjustments and picked out a few notes. Then she started to play, humming along to her notes, her fingers rippling up and down the frets of the guitar.

"Hey, she's good," Jesse pulled Caleb aside and whispered. "Maybe she would join our band?"

"We don't need another guitar player," Caleb responded.

"Sure we do. I can play bass," Jesse asserted. Caleb looked over at Kara who nodded her assent.

Ashley finished off with a slide down the bar then handed the guitar back to Caleb.

"Ask her," Jesse pushed Caleb in Ashley's direction.

"Not bad," Caleb said. "Where did you learn?"

"I had lessons." Ashley walked over to her bike and threw her leg over the inside bar. "It would have really rocked if we had electric guitars."

"Yeah, well, no electricity out here. This is the only place we have to practice."

"Too bad." Ashley put her foot on the pedal of her bike. Jesse glared at Caleb until Caleb put his hand on Ashley's bike.

"You want to play with us?"

"In your band?"

"Sure. What else?"

"Well, I don't know. It's not much of a band, practicing in the park. You don't even have a real set of drums."

"I have some at home. A little difficult to drag out here so I improvise," Kara explained.

"Look, if you're not interested, just say so." Caleb took his hand off of Ashley's bike.

"Maybe my dad would let us practice in our garage." Ashley took her foot off of the pedal.

"Does that mean you're in?" Caleb asked.

"That would be great. A new guitar player and a place to practice." Jesse came forward. "What do you say, Caleb?" he looked over at Caleb.

"It wouldn't hurt to try," Caleb responded.

"When do we start?" Ashley asked.

Chapter 35

"So, have you finally given up on your crusade against this place?" Gwen sighed as her feet were massaged. "I love pedicures."

"No, I'll just have to be more careful next time."

"I don't know what you are looking for. How do you prove someone is being held against their will if they don't speak your language to tell you? And even if they spoke the language, wouldn't fear keep them silent?"

Gwen's mother was better but still in the mental ward of the hospital. She had been told it would be several weeks before she would be better enough to come home. Marcie was glad her friend had a reprieve from her responsibilities, even though she knew it would be short-lived.

"Maybe so." Marcie saw the owner look in their direction. "We shouldn't be talking about this here."

"You said it yourself. These girls don't understand a word we say."

"Yes, but the owner does, and so does her creepy son. You want us to get kicked out?"

"And miss out on my weekly manicure, bi-weekly pedicure? No way."

Marcie looked at the manicure table were Mei-Lin was filing a client's nails. The last two times that Marcie had set up an appointment and asked for Mei-Lin, she had been told she wasn't available. What was up with that? She wished she had some way of communicating with her. The woman working on her feet had a rudimentary understanding of English, more than Mei-Lin, but she was busy chatting with the other salon worker who was rubbing Gwen's feet. Marcie tried to engage her in conversation.

"Do you speak English?"

"Yes, a little," she had told her. Marcie suspected she understood more English than she let on. When Marcie tried to get her to talk more, she said, "Boss no like," and looked over at the owner.

How do you find out if someone is being kept against their will if you can't communicate with them? One of the signs of trafficking, as well as any abusive situation, is isolation. The victim is kept away from anyone who might help them. The two girls working on her and Marcie's feet seemed happy enough, not like Mei-Lin, although they also had bruises hidden under their smocks. They appeared tough, hardened under the smiles they exhibited. There were two new workers today. They were even younger than Mei-Lin. Three girls had not been enough to keep up with all of the business. The owner had expanded the salon, knocking down walls to a room in the back that had been used as an office space and creating room for two more manicure tables, one more pedicure chair.

Marcie wondered where the new girls slept. Were they crowded into the space upstairs? The two older employees didn't appear too happy about the newcomers.

"You like nails?" her manicurist asked her as she polished Marcie's nails. The young woman looked at the owner who was occupied talking to a customer with her back to her. The owner's son was nowhere to be seen. "You help me," she whispered, "Get job so I can leave?"

"Are you in danger?" Marcie asked.

Lee smiled and said, "We love it here in America." Then she started chatting in Vietnamese to the other worker. Marcie saw the owner turn around and stare in their direction.

The owner came over and stood by Marcie. "Is everything satisfactory?"

"Yes. Lee was just telling me how much she loves it here."

"Too much idle chatter. She must bore you."

"I like talking to her." Marcie took a sip of her water bottle. "Business is booming, I see."

"Yes, it is good. Two more girls, more money, but more expense." The owner smiled then looked at Lee. "She must get her work done." Marcie took a gulp of water and started to cough.

"You mustn't drink so fast," the owner said and walked away.

Lee kept her head down while she did the final application. Without raising her head, with her lips barely moving, she said, "You help me?" then she raised her head and smiled. "All done. You like?"

"Yes," Marcie answered both questions. "I like."

"I don't care what anyone else says, there is something wrong with that woman. And her son is even worse." Marcie said once they were far enough away from the salon to not be heard by anyone.

"Why do you have to be so suspicious?"

"Lee asked me for help."

"She did?"

"Yes, while she was doing my nails. While the owner's back was turned."

"What are we going to do?"

"We?"

"I'm not going to let you do this alone."

That had been what Marcie had hoped Gwen would say. But what was she going to do? She had to have more proof than just Lee's request for help. She couldn't go back for another manicure till next week. Anything sooner would look suspicious. She thought the owner was wary of her as it was. If only there was some other way to communicate with Lee. And there was Mei-Lin to consider, and now two more girls. She would help Lee and the other girls in the process, but how?

"What if I told Lee I had a job for her? Maybe then she would leave the salon. Once out of the salon she would have no more reason to fear her boss. She could talk freely," Marcie suggested.

"But you don't have a job for her."

"No, but I bet we could get her one at one of the other salons in town."

"She'll need a place to stay. Do you think she could stay with you and your dad?" Gwen asked.

"Dad can't know about this. He told me to say out of it. What about your home?"

"What would I tell my dad?"

"That's true. We have to have a place for her. Maybe the women's shelter. She would be safe there." Marcie's mind raced as she sought out options.

"If they have space."

"They have to take her in if she's in danger, don't they?"

"I don't know."

"I'll check on it." Marcie made a mental note. The to-do list was growing longer.

"But what will happen to the rest of the girls once Lee is gone? Won't it be dangerous for them?"

Marcie hadn't thought of that. "We'll work something out. Let's sleep on it and see what other ideas we can come up with. We've got a week."

Marcie didn't say anything to Bernie about the plan forming in her brain. He was with her dad on this, had told her she should back off. "But he doesn't know I've been asked to help." She thought about talking to Pastor Joe about it but was afraid he would blow her off or tell her to stay out of it, like her dad.

"How do you know when to get involved and when to stay out of something?" she had asked him.

"And this is in regards to ...?"

"Nothing, nothing in particular."

"It can be hard to make those choices if you don't know the particulars. Those little details can make a world of difference," Pastor Joe said.

"Well, if you think someone is in trouble, how do you know when to interfere and when your interfering may cause more trouble?"

"Again, hard to say without knowing the particulars. This isn't about the Hello Kitty bike again?" Pastor Joe asked.

"No, not at all."

"Or the nail salon?" Pastor Joe stared intently at her.

"What if it were?" Marcie tried to avoid his gaze.

"Again, a hard one. What do you know?"

"What if someone asked for help?"

"Then I think there is some moral obligation to do something, if only telling someone else about the situation. What is this about, Marcie?"

"Nothing, boss, just a hypothetical."

"Then hypothetically speaking, if someone knows something that might endanger themselves or someone else, or if someone learns of a situation where someone is being harmed, then the proper authorities need to be notified. Hypothetically speaking that someone better be careful that they are not getting into something that they don't understand that can result in harm to self or others."

"Hypothetically speaking, of course."

"Of course. Marcie, what do you know? Maybe I can help."

"No, that's okay. That was all I was wondering about."

Chapter 36

Marcie and Gwen had their plan. They scheduled their usual manicures. Marcie didn't ask for Lee or Mei-Lin, lest Mrs. Chang be suspicious. She did ask who her appointment was with. When Mrs. Chang gave her a name she didn't recognize, she said. "Oh, I had hoped for Mei-Lin or maybe Lee."

"They are busy with other customers. Vee is a new girl, very good. You will like. I guarantee." Gwen was assigned to the other new girl.

"This will make it harder," Marcie conferred with Gwen. "How do we tell Lee about the job?"

"Chang watches like a hawk," Gwen commented.

"We'll think of something. If not, I guess we'll try again next week."

They were surprised when Lee wasn't even in the salon that next week.

"She has gone to visit her sister in Virginia," Mrs. Chang told them when they asked. "She be back next week."

"See," Gwen said as they left after their manicure. "If she is able to visit her sister, she is not a prisoner. Maybe we were wrong."

"Maybe, did you hear something?" Marcie heard what she thought was a rap on a window. "There, I heard it again." She looked up at the window above the salon and saw Lee quietly rapping to get their attention. Then they saw someone pull her away.

"She's not visiting relatives. She's in trouble, and I think it's because of us," Marcie said.

"What can we do? Call the police?"

"She might be dead before they get here. We have to do something. You call the police. I'll see if there is a back way up those stairs. Maybe I can cause a distraction." Marcie went to the back of the building while Gwen called 911 and told them about the situation. She went back behind the building looking for Marcie.

"Gwen, get over here," Marcie called from her hiding place behind the dumpster. "Someone's coming down the stairs." They watched as Mrs. Chang's son came out the door, holding Lee whose hands were tied behind her back, her mouth taped shut, her face visibly bruised. Behind her was another man, an American, one they had not seen before.

"We'll make an example of her," the American said. "It will be a lesson to the other girls."

Where are the police, Marcie thought, then without thinking, she grabbed a piece of two by four that had been left over from the remodeling and swung it at Chang and hit him on the head.

"Let her go," Marcie shouted. "Run, Lee."

"Foolish girl," the American said, "Do you want what she is getting? That can be arranged." He pulled out a gun. "Didn't your father teach you not to bring a bat to a gun fight? Tie her up," he instructed Chang. Chang had been hit hard but he had managed to hold onto Lee. He handed Lee over to the American and approached Marcie.

"Do you want another whack to your head?" Marcie threatened.

"Put the bat down." The American waved his gun at her. Just then a rock went soaring past Marcie hitting the American on the forehead. He staggered for a moment, startled by the blow, just enough to allow Lee to break free and run out to the street. Marcie tried to hit Chang again with the two by four, but this time he was prepared and stopped it mid-way. The American ducked the storm of rocks coming from behind the dumpster, reached behind it and dragged out Gwen.

"I guess these two will have to do," he told Chang. "Tie them up and put them in the car." Chang opened the trunk and was preparing to push the girls into it when they heard a voice.

"Police! Drop your weapons." An officer appeared in the alleyway. The American grabbed Gwen as a hostage.

"You're surrounded," another voice yelled as the first officer approached. "Drop your weapon." Another police officer came up behind the dumpster. "Let go of the girl. I'd just as soon shoot you as look at you," he added when the American hesitated.

The American let go of Gwen and put his weapon on the ground. The first officer grabbed it while two other officers put cuffs on Chang and the American.

"You two okay?" the first officer asked Marcie and Gwen.

"Yes," they said and continued holding each other up for support. Marcie recognized Officer Nash. "Thank you, Officer Nash," she added. Bernie pushed his way through the police line and hugged both girls.

"Are you okay? I came as soon as Gwen called."

"I take it you know him," Officer Nash said. "We've been casing this place for the past week, ever since we got the tip from Pastor Joe that something was going on. We have limited resources so we could not do around the clock surveillance. We suspected something big was coming down."

"Something big?" Marcie asked.

"A new shipment of girls. It's quite the racket. We were holding off to catch the ringleader. This guy here is one of them." He pointed at the American. "And this guy is a wannabe." He pointed at Chang.

"Are you saying we ruined your operation?" Marcie asked.

"No, not entirely at least. We still got the two of them, and you may have saved a life." He pointed to Lee who had been freed of her bonds and was under the care of paramedics.

"So, we did okay?"

"You did okay. In fact, it was your blog that first tipped us off. You've got good instincts."

In front of the salon, Mrs. Chang was being led off in handcuffs. The girls were being led out by Pastor Joe, Kathleen and some other officers.

"What's going to happen to them?" Marcie asked.

"They are going to get assistance through the Network Against Human Trafficking. They will find places for them to stay, help them apply for asylum," Officer Nash said.

"So, they will be okay?" Marcie asked.

"Thanks to you two." Office Nash indicated Gwen who was regaling a young officer with tales of her rock-throwing expertise.

"I always had a good arm for softball," Gwen said.

"Oh, and thank you for the tip about the runaway girl," Officer Nash added

"You mean the Hello Kitty bike?"

"Yes, turns out it was a runaway from a local foster home. Thanks to your blog, we were able to locate her and get her back into safe housing."

Marcie only half heard what Office Nash said. She watched as the girls were escorted to a van. Mei-Lin looked at Marcie for a moment. She didn't smile, she just looked. Marcie looked at her until she was in the van. She continued to watch as the van pulled away. If she had expected a sign of gratitude, she didn't get it, not from Mei-Lin or Lee, not from the other girls. She wondered, what had that child experienced? She was so young, and yet her eyes were so old.

Her stomach churned up into her throat. While Gwen had been excited and wanted to go out and talk about the adventure after being debriefed by the police, Marcie just wanted to go home.

"How can you go home after an afternoon like this?" Gwen asked.

"Please, Bernie, just take me home."

"Suit yourself," Gwen said then looked down at her nails. "Dang, I broke a fingernail."

Chapter 37

Her dad hadn't chided her or chastised her for her part in the raid. Her picture had appeared on TV during the local news that night. "Local girls help expose a human trafficking ring – News at eleven."

"Turn that off, Daddy," she said.

"You all right?"

"I guess. I think I'll go to bed." She didn't want to take any phone calls, didn't want to talk to any reporters, just wanted to sleep, but she couldn't. She tossed and turned all night. The emotionless face of Mei-Lin and the bruised face of Lee were embedded in her brain. When she did doze off, she saw the face of her grandfather, eyes red and glaring. She woke up in terror.

She didn't even bother to look at the tennis shoes dangling overhead as she rode her bike to work the next day.

"You sure you don't want me to drive you?" her dad had asked over breakfast.

"No, I'm okay," but she wasn't.

"That was foolish, what you did yesterday. You could have been killed," Joe said when he walked into the office. Marcie ignored him, as if lost in her work. He looked at what she was typing. Appeared to be the same paragraph over and over. "But, you saved a life. Maybe several lives. Good for you." Marcie burst into tears.

"What's wrong, Marcie?" Joe was used to crying women, but those were usually within the confines of his office or in hospital rooms. This was too much like dealing with his daughters.

"Here," he handed her a tissue, "come into my office where we can talk."

He allowed her to cry for a while as he wondered how long this would go on and what he would do when she stopped. When she seemed to be slowing down, he spoke.

"You did save a life yesterday, and even more lives. Who knows how many of those girls would have died had you not alerted the police and then taken the steps to help Lee."

"I guess."

"So then, why are you crying?"

"I don't know. Because I've messed up everything I've tried."

"What are you talking about?"

"All of the stuff I write, all the 'secrets', my blog, my sticking my nose into other people's business. I've found out things I never wanted to find out. Things I wish I could forget."

"Tell me more."

"Like the look on Mei-Lin's face when you took her away, the bruises on Lee's face," Marcie started to cry again, "the truth about my mother."

Joe pulled up a chair next to her and took her hands into his.

"And now, there's this creepy man, says he's my grandfather." Joe waited in silence, allowing the tears to slip down her face without rushing in to wipe them away.

"I wish I had never found out. I had this image of my mother in my mind. One I had made up years ago. How beautiful and kind and loving she was. I used to pretend to talk to her, tried to imagine what she was like, how she walked, the sound of her voice. When I needed advice, I would pretend she was talking to me. I pretended she was there at my birthday parties, all those years growing up, when I graduated from high school. Now, all that is gone, replaced by this woman I don't know, I don't want to know. I can't imagine the life she lived. My life has been so sheltered. To have grown up with that man. I can't fathom it. Don't want to understand because it hurts too much.

"And then to die the way she did. I wish I could go back to the beginning of the summer, to before I knew all of this. It just hurts too much, Pastor." Marcie looked over at him. "Do you think that sometimes people are hurt beyond repair? I mean, I've always heard that God never gives us more than we can handle, but are there some wounds that just can't be healed?"

Joe took in a deep breath as he thought how to respond. "I'm in the business of healing. I know I'd like to believe that there is nothing impossible for God. I've been taught that, I believe it and yet ... are there some emotional wounds that just can't be healed in this life? I believe so. I've seen people crushed by life circumstances, broken beyond repair, beyond my reach, my ability to heal them. But beyond God's ability? I don't know. Who are we to judge what is going on in another person's soul where they stand before their God? I don't. I believe God walks by their side in their struggle, in their pain, even in their poor choices, until the day God calls them home where they are healed, freed from all suffering and pain." Joe continued to hold Marcie's hands.

"I believe your mother was one such individual. Your dad told me about her. Did she make poor choices? Maybe, but I can understand why she made those choices, given her childhood. Perhaps it was a poor choice to leave you and your father, to not accept the help that was available to her to help her heal from the scars of her childhood. And yet, perhaps it was the best choice because, as you asked, some wounds are too deep to heal. She didn't want to hurt you or your father so she left. I know it may be hard to believe, but I trust that she made the best choice she could have made, that she made her choice out of love." Joe squeezed Marcie's hand as he spoke, looking at Marcie who looked away.

"So you don't have the perfect image of the perfect mother anymore." Joe said. "I think what you have is better. You have an imperfect mother who did what she felt she had to do to keep her daughter safe. That's better than any made-up image, isn't it?"

"It's so much to take in," Marcie continued to look down at her hands. "It hurts to think how much my mother suffered in her life."

"And yet she loved you enough to give you up." Joe put a box of tissues within her reach.

"I guess." Marcie wiped her eyes and runny nose. "I guess there's a reason why people have secrets. Some things are just best if not known."

"There are some secrets that are best kept hidden, kept between the persons involved. But others are best when shared. Not every secret is meant to be shared with everyone, only with those who have a right to know, a need to know. I think you needed to know the secret about your mother. It may be hard now, but you needed to know the human mother who loved you more than she loved herself." Joe paused as Marcie wiped the tears that had resurfaced as he spoke.

"Some secrets are best kept hidden, others are meant to be shouted from the roof tops," Joe continued. "Paul tells us the wonders of God's secrets, how Christ lives in each one of us, and about the glories in store for those who love God. How we will not die but rather be transformed. How God is transforming us even now. But perhaps the greatest secret is the secret of God's great love for us. It's a secret because we can't begin to comprehend how much our God loves us."

Marcie continued to cry into the tissues. "You know something of the Father's love because of the love you have received from your human father. And now you know something of your mother's love for you. And someday, maybe you will have a daughter and feel that powerful love, love that is willing to sacrifice itself for others. That barely scratches the surface of God's love.

"As you grow and love and live you will continue to grow in love for God and others if you are open to it. You will grow in understanding of God's love yet it will still remain a mystery, God's great secret."

Marcie blew her nose and wiped her tears. "I'm sorry. I'm a mess."

"Life is messy. That's as it should be. Messes are okay."

"I guess I better get back to work."

"No, you need to rest. You've been through some traumatic experiences the past few weeks. I'm taking you home and I want you to sleep all day and the next day and the next, if that is what you need. Don't come back to work until you are ready, truly ready to come back."

"But what about my bike?"

"That boyfriend of yours can pick it up in his truck. Or if not, it can stay here until you are ready for it."

Marcie barely made it out of Joe's car, when he dropped her off. He offered to help but she insisted she was okay. Joe watched as she stumbled up the stairs and into her home. Then he called Marcie's dad and Edna, his former secretary, not necessarily in that order.

Chapter 38

"You will help me celebrate my twenty-first birthday?" Gwen had called several times over the past few days, checking on Marcie's progress. She was relieved to hear Marcie's voice grow stronger.

"Of course. I'll be your designated driver," Marcie told her. She was back to work and feeling more like herself after her days of rest.

"Let's start at the Crab Shack then we'll decide from there. I can't wait to have a real cocktail, like a real grown-up adult! No more 'mocktails' for me."

Guess who's turning twenty-one today? Only the best friend a girl could have. If you know this newly legal to drink birthday girl, post your birthday wishes below. Marcie posted on her blog under a picture of Gwen from second grade. What Gwen didn't know was that everyone who responded was sent a separate message about a party at the Crab Shack that night.

"Where are you going?" Henry knew Marcie hated being asked where she was going when she went out, but Marcie also knew that was the price she paid for free room and board.

"The Crab Shack. They've got a band tonight. Then maybe we'll hit a couple bars. It's Gwen's first night of legal drinking."

"Call me if you need a ride."

"Don't worry, Dad. I'm the designated driver."

"Will Bernie be there?"

"Not at first, maybe later. Anything else?"

"I'd feel better if Bernie was going to be around. Call me if you need anything."

"Sure, Dad." Marcie was relieved to get out of the house. "My dad was being the grand inquisitor," she told Gwen as she climbed into Gwen's car.

"At least he cares enough to ask. I'm surprised my dad even remembered my birthday."

"He did give you a present, didn't he?"

"A gas card for my car. Dad's not too imaginative when it comes to gifts. Mom was always better at it than him."

"How is your mom?" Marcie had been unsure about bringing up the subject but since Gwen had mentioned her ...

"Okay. She's always okay when she's hospitalized. We'll see how she is when she comes home next week."

"That soon?"

"Her psychiatrist says she'll be ready."

"But will you be?"

"I guess I'll have to be. Let's not spoil my birthday talking about it." They rode in silence until Gwen pulled up to the Crab Shack. Outside stood a group of friends, wearing party hats and holding signs that said, "Happy Birthday, Gwen!" "The Big 2-1!" "Party-On!"

Gwen looked at Marcie, "Was this your idea?"

"Sure was." Marcie was grateful for the diversion to get Gwen's mind off of her mom. Gwen climbed out of the car and handed Marcie her car keys.

"Hey, where are my presents?" Gwen asked as a party hat was plopped on her head.

"Waiting for you inside. What better gift on a twenty-first birthday than a drink," Marcie said as she led Gwen in.

There was a band playing on the patio that night so the place was packed with people of all ages, cottage owners bored with the luxury of sunny days sitting on their porch enjoying the lake, boating and swimming, looking for alternative entertainment; and millennials looking for other millennials.

Being the designated driver was nowhere near as much fun as being able to drink. Marcie felt her mind wandering from the party. The jokes just weren't as funny when you were sober. And then there was that nagging feeling again that she was being watched. She wished Bernie would join them sooner, rather than later.

Marcie was pulled out onto the dance floor by Gwen into the middle of the group of friends. "Come on you party pooper! Nobody sits during my party. Everybody dances."

She felt herself loosen up as she joined the dancers, laughing as each took their turn dancing in the middle of the circle, each one more ridiculous than the last. She forgot her dis-ease as she danced, only to have it come rushing back as she saw that menacing face among the crowd, standing at the bar, beer in hand. He looked at her, tipped his beer and glared, the same glare she had seen at Jack's bar.

"Gwen, he's here." Marcie tried to get her friend's attention.

"Who?"

"Max."

"Where?" Marcie point to the bar, but he was gone. "You're imagining things, Marcie. Relax. Have a beer. It's my birthday."

"I know. That's why I'm the designated driver."

"One beer won't hurt." Gwen ordered a beer and gave it to Marcie. "It's my birthday. You have to drink it."

"Hey, Gwen, time for cake! Birthday cake cocktail! I had it made especially for you for your birthday." One of their friends pulled Gwen away.

"Woo-hoo!" Gwen said as she was led away. "I'm drinking my cake!"

Marcie sipped at the beer but wasn't willing to let down her guard. She continued to look about the crowded patio. The sun was setting, giving off a glow of pink over the water to the west. She decided to text Bernie.

"Come quick. Max is here." There, she thought, even if she was wrong, she would feel better if Bernie were here. When she felt her phone vibrate, she slipped outside of the crowded patio in order to be able to hear.

"Bernie," she said as someone grabbed her phone.

"Now don't you be calling no one, little lady," Max said as he grabbed her by the wrist, pulled her arm behind her back and started to push her away from the building. "And don't you be thinking about screaming or anything like that." He pressed something hard into her back. "Just come along quietly. Don't struggle none. You don't want my finger to slip on the trigger, do you?" Marcie stopped resisting and walked with him to the parking lot.

He reached into the back of the truck and pulled out some rope to tie her hands behind her back. "Now be a good girl and climb in that seat." Marcie saw a flash of metal in his right hand as he opened the door with his left. "Don't you be getting any ideas about running. It'd be a shame to hit such a beautiful girl on the head with the butt of this gun, but I will if I have to."

Marcie climbed in. "Do I have to tape that pretty little mouth shut?" he asked. Marcie shook her head no, unable to get any words out, much less scream as her throat tightened shut with fear.

"Good." Max shut and locked her door then climbed in the driver's side.

"Where are you taking me?" Marcie finally managed to get some words out of her throat.

"Where you belong. With me. We're going to some place where no one will find either of us. It will be our little secret." Marcie looked out the window. She didn't have to see him. She could imagine his lip raising in a sneer, revealing his gold tooth. "By the way, that's a nice little blog you got there."

Marcie looked over at him. "You read my blog?"

"How else did I find out about the birthday party for your friend? You should be more careful about sharing information." He smirked as he looked at the road ahead, pulling out of the parking lot of the Crab Shack. "We're going to my home."

Marcie could see the party continuing on the patio, oblivious to the fact that one member was missing. She wondered what Gwen would say when she realized she was gone.

"No one's coming to your rescue, little lady. You'll be long gone before those foolish friends of yours even realize you left the party." Marcie squirmed, trying to feel for her phone with her tied hands. "And if you are looking for this," Max held up her phone. "It's gone." He threw it out of the window into the lake as they drove away. "No one will be able to find you. No one will come to your rescue. Not even that bull-headed, miserly father of yours."

"My father will find me. He'll track you down. He knows all of the police in the county. They'll be looking for me."

"We'll be out of the county before he can notify them. If he hadn't been so cheap, none of this would be necessary."

"You won't get away with this, you know. No matter where you take me, he'll track you down."

"That so. We'll see about that. Now you sit back and ride quietly, lest I rethink my decision to not tape your mouth shut. We have a long way to go."

When Marcie's call was cut off, Bernie called Henry.

"I think something's wrong. Marcie texted me that she thought she saw Max. When I called her, she answered then we were cut off."

"Don't worry. I'm sure she's fine. Why don't you go to the Crab Shack and I'll do some checking," Henry tried to reassure Bernie and himself. Henry had had his private investigator tail Max and dig up as much dirt as he could. Last he knew Max had left town and was living in a trailer in the hills of Tennessee. He called Andy.

Gwen was frantic when Bernie showed up at the Crab Shack, looking for Marcie.

"Why she was right here the whole time," she insisted, embarrassed to admit that she had been having too much fun to notice that her best friend had gone missing.

"I think I saw someone who fits that description riding off in a truck with an old codger," one of the waitresses said when questioned. "I was taking a cigarette break. I thought it looked suspicious, that's why I noticed. But then you get all kinds of goings on here."

"You have to take me with you," Gwen insisted when their search revealed Marcie was nowhere to be found.

"I don't know where I'm going yet. Maybe you best get a ride home with one of your friends."

"No way." Gwen climbed into his truck, next to Blade. "I'm going with you."

"Just don't get in the way."

Gwen listened as Bernie talked to Marcie's dad.

"I'm not waiting. I've lived in Tennessee for the past five years. I know the area and have connections there. Give me the address." Bernie fumbled in the truck console for something to write with and write on. He pulled out a napkin from a previous drive-through meal. Gwen searched her purse for a pen and handed it to Bernie. She waited impatiently as Bernie started to write. "Yeah, I got it. I'm not familiar with that road." Bernie wrote some more.

"Okay. I know the area. Got a couple of buddies live out there. I'll call them. They might be able to help me find them." Bernie clicked off his phone and looked over at Gwen.

"Max's got a trailer somewhere in the woods of Tennessee," he told her. "Marcie's dad has alerted the police. They're putting out an alert for his truck. Chances are that's where he's going. Chances also are that he's going on back roads so as not to be noticed. Anyway, that's where I'm headed. You better go home."

"You're not going anywhere without me." Gwen stated, refusing to leave the truck.

Marcie willed herself to stay awake during the drive. She wanted to know where she was going so that if the opportunity came and she got to a phone, she would be able to tell her dad where she was. She found herself thinking about her blog. What a mistake it had been.

"You just relax, little one. Try to get some sleep," Max said. He looked over at Marcie as she struggled to keep her eyes open. He reached out and caressed her face. Marcie pulled away, moving as far away from him as she could.

"Now you and me are gonna be good friends. No need to fight it." He patted his gun then put his hand back on the wheel. "You're pretty. As pretty as your mama was. Slut that she was. She was no good, sleeping around."

Marcie watched him from her corner of the truck cab.

"But you're a good girl. I can see that. Even with that no-good cowboy slinking around. We'll get up to my trailer then take to the woods. No one will find us there. If your daddy wants you back, he'll have to do what I say, uppity attorney. I never had no use for attorneys."

"I have to use the bathroom," Marcie interrupted his stream of conversation.

"You'll just have to hold it until I say you can go."

"But I have to go now."

"I know your tricks. You just want me to untie you so you can go inside and lock the door and not come out. No, if you have to go, we'll pull off by the side of the road and I'll pull down your panties for you."

"I can wait." Marcie tried to slide even further against the truck door.

"I thought so."

They drove all night. They drove through small towns with names she had never heard of. All she could tell was that they were somewhere in Tennessee when Max pulled off onto a gravel road. They drove a short way, then Max turned again onto a narrow dirt path. They had only gone a few feet when Marcie heard voices.

"You going somewhere, Mister?" Marcie was surprised when two men with shot guns appeared next to the truck. They had driven all night without seeing one cop, one roadblock. She expected her dad had called the cops. So where were they, she wondered. She was afraid once Max was in the hills of Tennessee they would never find her. And now these two hillbillies ...

"Just driving to my trailer up a-ways."

"This is private property. Who said you could park your trailer up there?"

"Why this is public property. These hills don't belong to nobody."

"But this land you are driving through does." Marcie could see Max's hand on his gun, pointing it in her direction.

"And who might this lady be?" One of the men approached Marcie's side of the truck.

"That's my granddaughter. She's come to visit for a while – right, honey?"

Marcie muttered, "Yes."

"Speak up, child. Let the men hear you."

"Yes," Marcie stated.

"That so. Maybe we want to see for ourselves. Why are your hands behind your back?"

"You tell them, honey. Tell them it's all right."

"I'm fine." Marcie looked away from Max to the man with the shot gun. She didn't know which would be worse.

"This man your grandfather?"

"Yes, he is."

"All right then. Maybe we'll let you pass."

"Thank you kindly," Max said.

The men stepped aside. Max drove through slowly. "You did right good, little lady. We'll be there soon. Once we reach the trailer I'll pack some food and we'll be gone. No one will find us."

Marcie and Max rode for almost an hour before reaching the trailer, or so it seemed to Marcie.

"No use in running. You'll be lost for weeks in these woods before anybody finds you, if they ever find you. Be eaten by a bear before you could find the main road." Max pulled up to the trailer, let Marcie out and untied her hands. "Now make yourself useful. Get us some water." He pointed to a pump a short way from the trailer. "You know how to pump water, don't you?" He pulled her over to the pump, poured some water sitting in a can next to it into the pump to prime it then started pumping until water flowed.

"Here," he handed Marcie a bucket. "Fill this, then bring it in. Don't be trying anything foolish. I'll have my gun on you. Besides you don't want to take no chances with those bears."

Marcie did as she was told, pumping water into the bucket while she surveyed the area. He was right. She had no idea where she was or how to get out. She could tell which way was north, south, east and west, but that didn't do her any good. The path had turned so many times on the way there. She didn't know which way would lead her out of the woods. She couldn't use the road. He would find her there.

She heard a vehicle coming up the road and thought she recognized the men with the shot guns. Time to get away. The unknown in the woods couldn't be worse than what she knew awaited her if she stayed, she told herself. When Max went out of the trailer and approached the truck, she saw her opportunity and ran for it. Down a tree covered ravine, up again, into the thick underbrush of woods. She ran without heeding any sound but her own breathing.

Chapter 39

Bernie looked over at Gwen. Blade was sleeping with his head on her lap. She was struggling to keep her eyes open, her head nodding then jerking back up right.

"You might as well get some sleep if you can. It'll be morning by the time we get there."

"No, I'm fine. I'll keep you company." They rode in silence as Gwen's head continued to bob up and down. "I've got to pee," Gwen finally said. "Sorry. Too much beer. I don't mean to slow you down."

"Don't worry. We have to stop for gas soon anyway. He got a head start on us, but we'll be making better time since we are taking the highway. Like I said, I think he's driving back roads to avoid attention. My buddies down there will head them off. I already called them." Bernie stopped then added, "Oh, and happy birthday."

"Some birthday. My best friend gets kidnapped while I'm drinking. It's my fault. I should have listened to her when she said she saw Max."

"It's not your fault. If not today, it would have been some day. Just a matter of time. I suspect he's been waiting his time for the right opportunity."

"I guess."

"You never liked me much, did you?" Bernie changed the subject.

"I love you, man, but you're not much of a boyfriend."

"What do you know about it?"

"I just know you broke my friend's heart and will again. Marcie may forgive you, but I don't. Besides, every time you were around, I was the third wheel."

"I'm sorry you felt like that."

"Don't be. It happens. I guess I didn't like sharing my best friend with you."

"And now?"

"Now I'm kind of glad you're around. But you'll be gone again and I'll have to pick up the pieces."

"Is that what you think?"

"It's true, isn't it? You'll be off with that band of yours, leaving Marcie heart-broken again."

"I do have to leave. Marcie understands that."

"Well, Marcie forgives you. Why should I forgive you?"

"You saying I have to earn your forgiveness?"

"Damn straight. Wait. Stop the car." Gwen's head was swimming. Bernie pulled over. Gwen jumped out on the side of the road.

"You okay?" He looked through the door Gwen had left open and waited for Gwen to climb back in.

"Now I really need that bathroom to get cleaned up."

"We'll be there soon." Bernie rolled the window down a crack to bring in fresh air.

"Sorry," Gwen said as her head rolled back against the seat.

"Thank you for not throwing up in my truck." Bernie looked over at her, her head leaning against the door, her mouth left open and a slight snore coming from her. Blade moved closer to Bernie and put his head on his lap.

"That's okay, boy." Bernie rubbed the dog's ears as he drove off the highway to a truck stop. "She won't remember a thing when she wakes up."

"Okay, keep an eye on them. I'll be there in an hour or so." Bernie responded to the phone call.

"Can't you play anything besides that darn country crap?" Gwen stated as she woke up. "What time is it?"

"Six o'clock."

"Whoa, my head hurts. One too many birthday drinks. What am I doing in your truck? Are you kidnapping me?"

"No, remember? Marcie was kidnapped. By her grandfather. Remember. You insisted on coming along."

"Oh, yeah, I think I remember. Tell me again what happened."

"Here, I got you some coffee at the last stop. Drink up. And there's aspirin in my glove compartment."

"Thank you." Gwen accepted the coffee and fumbled to get the glove compartment open. "You come prepared."

"You might say this isn't my first rodeo."

Gwen fumbled to get the childproof cap off of the aspirin. "What are you talking about?"

"You're not the first drunk to be in my truck. I'm always prepared. Right Blade?" Bernie reached over and scratched the dog's ears again. He had sat up when Gwen started talking.

"So, what are we doing next? Damn," Gwen swore as she spilled coffee on her front.

"At least it smells better than barf."

"Did I throw up last night?" Gwen knew the truth as the taste still lingered in her mouth and the smell on her clothes.

"Only once, and you were kind enough to get out of my car to do it. Not everyone is that considerate."

"Sorry." Gwen tried to wipe the coffee with a napkin that had been in the container with the coffee. "I'm so sorry. I've blown everything. My birthday was a fiasco. I'm such a loser, throwing up in your truck, and I look like an idiot," she looked down at the stained party dress, "and smell like a wino."

"More like beer."

"You know what I mean. Meanwhile my best friend is missing."

"You had nothing to do with that."

"I should have been with her. I should never have let her out of my sight. I should have listened to her when she said she thought she saw her grandfather. Instead I was too caught up in having fun." Gwen took another sip of coffee. "What do we do now?"

"I've got some friends looking out for them. They just saw them. They are going to follow them, keep a look-out."

"Then what's taking us so long. Get moving. Put the pedal to the metal."

"That's what I've been doing all night while you slept. We have to be careful now. Don't want to spook him. They said he has a gun on Marcie." Gwen stopped drinking as the information sunk in. "This is not a game, any more than that time at the nail salon," Bernie told her.

"Why does Marcie keep getting into these situations? And how come you're so calm?"

"I'm not calm. I'm wired from too much coffee, no sleep and eight hours of driving. But rushing in is not going to help Marcie and may just get her killed."

Gwen's voice cracked and tears formed. "And it's all my fault."

"Don't start again. We don't have the time or luxury for self-pity right now."

"So what do we do?"

"My friends know the woods like the back of their hands. They'll keep an eye on them till we get there."

"And then what?"

"I don't know. Guess we'll figure it out as we go. Marcie's dad has contacted the local police and the FBI. He's on his way down. Told me to wait for him."

"But you won't."

"What do you think?"

"I guess you are a good person to have in an emergency." Gwen paused before continuing. "Marcie told me about your family situation. About your mom and all. I'm sorry."

"Yeah, well, she told me about your mom, too."

"Seems we have more in common than just Marcie."

"Seems we do," Bernie said as he focused on the road ahead.

Chapter 40

Marcie didn't know where she was going, just that she wanted to get as far away from that trailer as possible. She thought she may have heard gunshots but was afraid to stop to find out. She believed that she was running in the general direction of the road, but when she had been running for twenty minutes and couldn't see it, she stopped and thought about changing course. Her sandals were not the best for running, but at least afforded some protection from sticks and stones she encountered as she ran.

"Wait a minute," she told herself. "You can't keep running like this." She was surprised that she didn't hear anyone scouring the woods looking for her. What had happened to her grandfather? Maybe those men had shot him. What would they do to her? She looked at the sun and tried to get her bearings. Her grandfather had turned north off of the highway when he went on the dirt road. If she went south, then eventually she would have to reach the road, right, as long as no bears got her first. She plotted out her course and began walking. As the sun rose higher she realized how hungry and thirsty she was. "If only I had brought some water," she thought. But no, there had been no time for water. She had had to run as soon as she saw her opportunity.

As she paused to think, she thought she heard something moving, coming in her direction. Just my imagination, she thought at first. Or a squirrel. The woods were full of them. Or an opossum. As she listened the sound grew louder, coming in her direction. A random squirrel wouldn't be coming straight for her, would it? The noise was louder than what a squirrel would make. Definitely bigger than a squirrel and it was headed in her direction. What if it was a bear? Could she outrun it? No, she had to find a safe place, climb a tree. She looked around for a climbing tree. Nothing. Her mind, exhausted from lack of sleep and nutrition, wouldn't function.

She started to run, no longer worrying about whether she was going north or south, when she tripped over a limb and landed flat on the ground. Her foot caught in the branch and twisted, leaving her in pain. The noise grew louder and closer. Her mind raced. All of the lost opportunities, all that she had dreamed of doing someday, was that all going to end in a secluded forest? Will anyone even find her or will she be an unsolved mystery, a cold case? If only she had more time, time to tell her dad how much she loved him. Time with Bernie and Gwen.

The noise grew even closer and landed on her before she could get up, as she felt a wet tongue lick her face.

"Blade? How did you find me?" Blade continued to lick her. "And where is your master?" Marcie hugged the dog, nuzzling into his neck. "I knew you would find me," she whispered into his floppy ear.

Chapter 41

Marcie knew that wherever Blade was, Bernie couldn't be far behind. Sure enough, she heard his familiar voice calling out for her, along with another familiar voice.

"Here. I'm here!" she yelled back. "I knew you would come," she told Bernie as he wrapped her in his arms.

"Don't forget about me," Gwen said as she arrived, struggling to run in her skirt and sandals.

"And you, too. How did you find me?"

"It was a team effort," Bernie said as Gwen hugged her friend.

"Phew! You reek," Marcie laughed. "What is that? Eau de coffee and barf?"

"You don't exactly smell sweet yourself," Gwen said as she hugged Marcie back, the smell of sweat engulfing her.

"Your dad had hired a private investigator to keep track of your grandfather. He knew about this trailer and I have friends who know these woods."

"The men with the shot guns?"

"Yeah. They're buddies of mine." They heard more voices in the woods calling her name. "Your dad's got the whole local Sheriff Department and the FBI scouring the woods for you. Over here!" Bernie called out. A deputy joined them.

"They're here. We've located the girl," he radioed.

"She safe?" a voice asked.

"Appears to be, except for a twisted ankle. Tired and thirsty but other than that, okay."

"Can she walk?"

"You up to walking?" he asked Marcie.

"Anything. I can handle anything after last night."

"Head on back to the trailer," the voice said.

Marcie walked with Bernie and Gwen on either side, supporting her through the woods. Blade led the way back to the trailer.

Her dad rushed to greet her, squeezing her into a bear hug. "Are you okay, baby? I never should have let you out of my sight. Not as long as that man was still around."

"I'm okay, Dad. I twisted my ankle, but it's not bad. I can walk on it."

"We'll have it checked out, no arguments."

"But how did you find me?"

"Andy, my private investigator." Her dad pointed Andy out and motioned for him to join them. "He's been watching Max. Last we knew he was down here. We were checking on other warrants for his arrest, figured someone like him couldn't have gone this long without perpetrating another crime. Not once your mom and grandma were gone."

Andy spoke up. "For the most part he had stayed under our radar, but there was a marriage to a sixteen-year-old. We didn't find much till we found his aliases. He changed his name several different times. We found warrants under each name."

"We thought maybe he had given up on you, but instead he was just biding his time to put us off guard," her dad added. "We were getting ready to have him picked up."

"Where is he? Was he shot? I thought I heard gun shots."

"Nope. What you heard was us, just knocking a little sense into your granddaddy's head." The two men with shot guns came forward.

"These are the friends I told you about," Bernie told her. "Rich and Logan."

The two took off their hats and nodded at Marcie when introduced. Rich was the older of the two. Marcie guessed he was in his thirties. Logan appeared to be Bernie's age or younger.

"Sorry if we scared you, ma'am," Rich said. "We could see that he had a gun on you. We didn't want to spook him any. Wanted to make sure you were safe before going after him."

"How did you get him?"

"We talked to him for a while once he came out of the trailer to make sure there was no one else around. When we figured he was alone, we pulled out our rifles and Logan here fired a round just to let him know we were serious."

"We asked him where you were but when he looked you had already run off. So, we tied him up and waited for Bernie to get here," Logan added.

"That's how I found them. Your dad and the rest were right behind me. While they made plans to systematically search the woods," Bernie pointed in the direction of the sheriff and FBI agents, "I sent Blade after you. Best hound dog around." Bernie reached down and hugged the dog while Marcie sat on a stump, taking it all in. "I knew he would find you. The rest you know."

"What you don't know is how lucky you are, young lady," the sheriff said. "It looked like your grandfather was going to go off the grid. He had weeks' worth of supplies packed in the trailer. Once he got you out in those woods, it would have been close to impossible to find you."

"Let me look at your ankle," one of the deputies wrapped her ankle. "Doesn't appear to be broken. Still wouldn't hurt to have it checked out."

"What happens now?" Marcie asked, looking over at Max.

"You don't have to worry about him. With his priors and now this, he'll be in jail for a long time, where people like him belong," the sheriff told her.

"We will need you to testify," the FBI agent said. "And we need to get your statement when you are ready."

"I think the first thing we need to do is get these ladies to a place where they can shower, get cleaned up and get something to eat. You too, young man. Thank you for all your help," Henry said to Bernie. "And your friends, too. Have a meal on me," he said to Bernie's friends, then placed his hand on Marcie's shoulder. "And we have to get that ankle checked out."

"Just so you don't leave before giving me a statement," the agent said.

"That won't happen. You have my word on it. I want that man in jail even more than you do," Henry said. Henry got rooms for Marcie and Gwen and him and Bernie. While they showered, he picked up some clean clothes for the girls. They had a long, late lunch, lingering until they could hardly keep their eyes open, then went back to their rooms and fell fast asleep.

"You awake?" Marcie asked Gwen later that night.
"Huh?"
"You awake?"
"I am now." Gwen rolled over and looked at Marcie.

"I'm sorry about ruining your birthday."

"What do you mean, you're sorry? I mean, I got to go on a road trip with a country singer and his dog, took part in a woman hunt, and met some pretty cute country boys along with some deputies and an FBI agent. Who could ask for a better birthday? All future birthdays will be compared unfavorably to this one. You have set the bar awfully high, Marcella Taylor."

"I'm glad you had so much fun at my expense."

"You're welcome." Gwen turned back over. Marcie laid on her back staring at the ceiling.

"So, road trip with Bernie. Are you saying you're friends now?"

Gwen rolled on her back and stared at the ceiling as well. "Well, I don't know that you'd call us friends, but I guess he's okay."

"Only okay?"

"Hey, he's your boyfriend, not mine. I guess I can see what you see in him, maybe. Is that enough?"

"Yes, that's enough."

"Now can I sleep?"

"I don't know. I wanted my two best friends to be friends, but now that it has happened ..."

Gwen threw a pillow at her. "You are never satisfied, aren't you?"

"I guess not."

"Well, get off the fence. It's too late to change your mind now that you have thrown us together. Now go to sleep. I need my beauty rest."

Marcie continued to stare at the ceiling as Gwen snored in the background.

Chapter 42

"So," Kathleen looked over at Joe over dinner. Joe knew that look. "Do you have any secrets you aren't telling me?"

"What? What are you talking about?"

"I was just thinking about that blog on secrets. Is there anything you are keeping from me?"

"Of course not. What do you want to know? Just ask and I'll tell you." Why did Joe suspect a set-up?

"Don't lie to me. Everybody has secrets. What are yours?"

"You tell me yours first."

"I think you know them already. You know way too much about me." Kathleen picked at her salad.

"And you know about me." Joe tried to avoid the trap he knew was being set for him.

"Not enough. I want to know more. Come on, tell me. You have to have a few delicious secrets to share. A past tryst or two. A secret love or indiscretion. What about all the secrets others share with you?" Kathleen insisted.

"Those are not for me to share."

"So, come up with some secrets of your own."

"Okay, but if I tell you something, then you have to tell me one too."

"Deal."

"Okay," Joe paused before continuing. He knew he could no longer avoid the trap. "It's no secret how much I love you, but what you don't know is how your eyes crinkle when you smile and how wide they get when you are lying."

"That's no secret. I want something better."

"Then, how about that I had a friend in the Chicago police force do some checking on you after I first met you."

"You did what?"

"I checked up on you. After all, Stephanie was hanging out with your son, Scott. I had to know more about you."

"You sneak. You never told me."

"There was no reason to tell you. I found out what I wanted to know, then I got to know you myself." Joe knew that would not be the end of it but he still hoped to divert her. "Now you tell me one."

"And here I thought you were so good and trusting of others, giving them the benefit of the doubt."

"Not when that someone's son is hanging out with my daughter. I was protecting my daughter."

"And who's to protect me from you, you holier-than-thou hypocrite?"

"You started this. You were the one who insisted on sharing secrets. Now what about yours?"

"It seems you know all my secrets already. You and your cop friend."

"I did give you the benefit of the doubt, even after I knew your history."

"I knew you would throw it in my face someday."

"I'm not throwing it in your face. You are the one who started this whole thing."

"Then maybe I should end it." Kathleen got up and prepared to leave. "It's a good thing we kept this relationship a secret. No one to tell once it's over."

Joe stopped her. "You still owe me a secret."

"That's for me to know and you to find out, assuming, of course, that you don't already know."

"Yeah, well here's another secret, you're a lousy cook."

Kathleen slammed the door. "Infuriating man," Joe heard her mutter as she let herself out.

"Infuriating woman," Joe thought. Still he wondered at how beautiful her eyes were when flashing sparks. What other secrets did they hold?

Kathleen had calmed down by the time she got home. Her mother and stepfather were in the front room with the TV on.

"You know, Mom, what I said before about not realizing about you and your boyfriends."

"Yes?" Esther looked up from the afghan she was knitting. Peter was tilted back in a lounge chair snoring.

"I lied. I knew what I was doing."

"I know that." Esther continued to knit.

"What do you mean? You knew I was purposefully chasing those men away?"

"Honey, it was so obvious. You weren't ready to have a new man in the house. I could tell that. Besides, you were a good judge of men, or perhaps you were the litmus test. If they could get through you, then I figured maybe they were worth keeping around."

"So, no one passed my test?"

"No. Perhaps I didn't want them to. No one passed until Peter." Esther nodded in Peter's direction. Peter buck-snorted but continued to sleep.

Kathleen laughed. "Yep, he's a keeper."

"And Joe. He's a good one, too."

"I don't know. He's still a stuffed shirt."

"There's an awfully fine man under that shirt."

"If you say so." Kathleen shrugged her shoulders. "You know, let's not keep anymore secrets. We're too old for that."

"Are we? But what fun would that be?" Esther and Kathleen both laughed. Peter snorted again and woke himself up

"What's so funny?" he asked.

"Nothing, dear." Esther smiled as she went back to her knitting.

Back when Stephanie and Scott were going to school together, there were more excuses for Joe and Kathleen to run into each other. Joe was still on the board of the Center for the Arts, but meetings were monthly. That was way too long in between. How to casually bump into Kathleen, Joe wondered? He wasn't going to come crawling back to her. That was for sure, but he did want to get back together. She didn't go to church, so they couldn't run into each other there. He was surprised when his phone rang and he saw a familiar name.

"We on for dinner tomorrow?" Kathleen asked.

"Why, yes, I guess so. If you still want to."

"Why wouldn't I? It's our regular date night."

"I thought after last night ..."

"My turn to cook. Don't worry, my mom is making enough for all of us. You won't have to suffer through any more of my cooking."

"But what about last night? I thought you didn't want to see me."

"Oh, that. I thought it over. And, besides I did some checking on you, too."

"You did?"

"Sure. I've got connections too, you know. Awfully suspicious why a pastor in the prime of his life would leave a large church in a growing metropolis for a smaller church in nowheresville. I had to make sure there were no skeletons in your closet forcing you to move. No unnatural interest in teenage boys or other weird stuff."

"What?"

"It doesn't matter. You were clean. Just because you were a man of the cloth didn't give you a free pass. Let's just call it even."

"I guess."

"Let me make it up to you with one of my mom's home-cooked meals."

"Really, you are not cooking?"

"I promise."

"Then it's a deal."

Chapter 43

"You know I have secrets too," Ashley said on the drive to her grandma's. Sleep-overs at her grandma's with her Aunt Kathleen had been a regular part of her weekends since her mom had died. She no longer went for a night every weekend but Kathleen made sure they got together at least once a month.

"Oh, you do? Tell me," Kathleen gave Ashley a conspiratorial grin. She was surprised when Ashley didn't respond in kind. Was surprised at how serious Ashley had become.

"I killed my mom," Ashley whispered.

"What are you talking about? Your mom died of cancer. You know that."

"But I wanted her to die," Ashley wiped away the tear that slid down her face. "She was so sick all the time and she didn't have time for any of us and everyone was so sad. I wanted it to be over."

"Ashley, honey, you were just seven years old when your mother died."

"I was almost eight," Ashley corrected her.

"You weren't much older than Grace. Don't you think your mom knew you loved her?"

"And I was so mean to her at the end. I didn't want to hug her. I didn't want to be with her. It hurt too much."

"Your mother understood all of that. She loved you so much."

"And I love her, but now she will never know how much because I didn't tell her."

Kathleen pulled the car over to the side of the street and reached over to hug Ashley. "Your mom knows you love her."

"How can she? She's gone."

"She knows. I wasn't nice to my dad before he died. I had been angry at him. I had felt guilty about that for a long time. But now I know he understood, that he knew and knows I love him. My dad is still with me in ways I don't always understand, but he is." Kathleen had been four when her father had died in an accident. "Your mother is still with me. I miss her very much. And I know that she is with you, too, that she understands. Do you believe that?"

"I don't know. That's what Pastor Joe says too, but what does he know."

"I suspect he knows more than either of us imagine. He was close to your mom at the end of her life." Kathleen gave Ashley another hug. "I'm sorry you've been carrying this secret alone for so long. I'm really happy that you trusted me enough to tell me. You will tell me if anything more comes up, won't you?"

"I guess. Sometimes I don't know myself until something happens."

"I know about that." Kathleen started the car again. "How about we see what your grandma has prepared for dinner? And afterwards, we'll have ice cream, my treat."

"Pastor?" Marcie stopped Joe before he could make it to his office.

"Marcie?"

"I've been wondering about what you had said."

"About what?"

"About the secret of God's love."

"And ...?" Joe had been in a hurry to get to his office before his first appointment.

"Well, I mean, it seems to me it's no secret. Everybody knows about it." Marcie was sitting at her desk. Joe turned away from his path to his office.

"But do they really believe it? Do they really believe that God loves them, personally? And if so, can they even begin to realize just how much God loves them?"

"I don't know."

"My experience is that most people don't have the slightest inkling about the depth of God's love."

"Then what about my mom?"

"What do you mean?"

"If God loved her so much, how could God have let her suffer so? I only spent a night with her father and that was more than I could take. I can't imagine being stuck with him for all those years." Marcie remained seated at her desk. Joe walked over closer to her and sat down across from her.

"Maybe the question isn't how much God loved her, but whether she was able to accept that love." Joe leaned toward Marcie. "There's so much that I don't understand. I don't understand why there is so much suffering in this world, but I do believe that God loves us. I believe God loved your mom and was right there with her in all of her pain and hurt. God even loves your grandfather, though how God can is beyond me to understand. It's all part of the mystery of God's love. Does that help?"

"I don't know how anyone can love that man. Not even God."

"I find that hard too, but I believe God does. God knows secrets we can't begin to understand. God knows your grandfather and all of his secrets, secrets that have made him the man he is. And God loves him anyway."

"I'll never understand a God that can love someone like him, a God who allows vulnerable children to be harmed, abused."

"You don't have to understand God to believe in God, to love God."

"I guess not." Marcie shook her head. "You're going to be late for your appointment." Joe looked at her, realizing he had just been dismissed.

"Are you sure you're okay."

"Sure, now go."

Later that morning Marcie called through the intercom, "Pastor, it's Jeremy Long on the phone. He sounds upset."

"Put the call through." Minutes later Pastor Joe came out of his office. "I'm going to the hospital. Mrs. Long is there."

"Is it serious?"

Marcie saw the look on Pastor Joe's face. She recognized that look. She figured he was trying to decide how much to tell her? Yes, it was common knowledge that Janet Long had recently given birth to their sixth child. She had been sent home, but from the tone of Mr. Long's voice on the phone she suspected something wasn't right.

"I don't know. She might have pre-eclampsia."

"Pre-eclampsia?"

"Yes, a life-threatening complication with some pregnancies. Usually it occurs before the birth but sometimes symptoms can occur after the mother has been sent home from the hospital."

"Is there anything I can do? Who's taking care of the children?"

"Other family members are watching the children."

"Then what can I do?"

"Pray, just pray," Pastor Joe said as he went out the door.

This wasn't the first time Pastor Joe had been called away for an emergency. There were people in crisis, people in tears in and out of his office. People with money problems, people battling addictions, all fighting their own particular demon. She didn't know how Pastor Joe did it. She was discovering a new respect for him. She knew she couldn't do what he did.

He called shortly before three o'clock. "Mrs. Long didn't make it." Marcie noted the tiredness in his voice. "The funeral will be sometime this weekend. Would you contact the funeral dinner team and the bereavement team?"

"I will. Anything else?"

"No, that's enough for now. I'll see you tomorrow."

Suddenly her own problems seemed so much less.

Chapter 44

Dale was uncomfortable as he escorted Ava into the church office. He didn't know why. He had come here many other times, with and without Ava. Why did this time feel different, he wondered?

"Aren't you Ashley's parents?" the church secretary asked.

"I guess our fame has preceded us," Dale joked. "Yes, we are. And you're Marcie."

"You aren't going to put us in your blog, are you?" Ava asked.

"Not unless you want me to. Do you? Want me to write about you, that is?" Marcie responded.

"No. Being Ashley's parents is enough fame for us," Dale said.

"That's good, because I'm not supposed to be writing about church members anyway." Marcie led them to Pastor Joe's office and left.

"So how are you two doing?" Joe asked as they sat on the couch and he sat down in the chair across from them.

"We're fine. How's Ashley?" Dale was the first to speak. Ava reached over and placed her hand on his as he spoke.

"You know I can't tell you what we talk about," Joe responded.

"I know, but you can tell me how she is doing, can't you?"

"What have you noticed?" Joe turned the question back on Dale. Dale looked over at Ava before speaking.

"She seems to be better, happier. Don't you think so, honey?"

Ava nodded her head in agreement. "She's not as sulky."

"Moodiness is normal for teen girls. I raised two, though how I did it, I still wonder."

"I know. I was a teen girl once myself," Ava said. "But she does seem better. She still doesn't talk much, at least not to me."

"Or me," Dale added.

"It's hard, trying to blend families," Joe noted.

"But I don't have any kids," Ava stated.

"Yes, but you are a newcomer to an already established family. How is that going?"

"Okay, but," Ava looked over at Dale before continuing, "The kids don't really listen to me."

"I tell them to listen," Dale interrupted.

"I know you do, but you're not there all the time, especially now that school's out. Ashley's the worst. I thought I knew something about handling kids her age, since I teach that age group. But it's not the same as being a parent. What works in the classroom doesn't always work in a home."

"There's a learning curve for all of you," Joe said. "Most step families take as long as five years or more to gel as a family."

"That long?" Ava looked over at Dale again. Dale figured he knew what she was thinking: What had she gotten herself into? "I don't know if I can wait that long."

"It will take as long as it takes. But there are things you can do to help." Joe started to write on a piece of paper. "The church has a support group for step families. You may want to check them out. Here's the contact person." Joe held out the paper.

Ava looked at Dale, waiting for him to speak. "That's okay, Pastor. We are fine. We don't need a support group," Dale said.

"Maybe not now, but why not take the info, just in case." Dale accepted the paper and put it in his pocket.

"Back to Ashley," Joe redirected the conversation. "Have you considered getting her her own room? It can be hard for a twelve-year-old girl to share her room with a seven-year-old sister."

"I said the same thing," Ava looked over at Dale again.

"We don't have the room," Dale said. "Grace can't move in with Jacob. Ashley will just have to learn to get along with Grace."

"Just a thought," Joe said. "Anything else?"

"No, well ..." Dale shifted on the couch and bounced his right leg. Ava reached over and placed her hand on his knee till it stopped. "Do you think we didn't wait long enough before getting married?"

"You mean as far as the kids are concerned? For kids, I don't know that there is ever an optimal time to remarry, unless, of course, you wanted to wait until they were grown and out of the house, but even then it takes time. Even grown children can struggle with a new member of the family."

"No, I mean for us. Did we rush into this? Should we have waited longer?" Dale asked.

"At this point, I don't think it matters either way," Joe responded.

"I want to know what you think, Pastor," Dale continued.

Joe paused before answering. "I don't think you rushed into this without thinking. I don't think you married Ava before getting over Joy sufficiently. Sufficiently is the key word here. Do you ever get over the loss of someone you love? Not entirely, but you do move on. You have moved on sufficiently to be open to love again. Joy would have wanted you to marry again." Joe looked at both of them.

"I know both of you. There are no guarantees in life. But I think you've got as good a chance of making it as a couple as the next couple, maybe an even better chance because you know what you want," Joe looked at Dale, "and what you don't want in a marriage," he turned his gaze to Ava.

"So, no, you didn't rush into marriage. And if there is still healing to do from both of your previous marriages, I believe you have the ability to do that together. You can support each other in any healing that needs to happen."

Joe waited for either of them to respond. When they didn't, he continued, "Marriage can be a crap shoot."

"Pastor," Ava looked at him with surprise. Dale chuckled.

"I've seen marriages I thought for sure would go the distance, good communication skills, shared values, end in divorce. And others I thought didn't have a chance that are still together twenty years later. No one knows what goes on in a marriage, except the couple, and even they are often clueless. It's a secret, one worth exploring."

"Is that why you haven't remarried yourself?" Dale asked, a grin creeping up around the edges of his mouth.

"That's for me to know." Joe said and stood up. "I believe our time is up."

Dale and Ava rode in silence for a few blocks. Ava was the first to break the silence.

"A teenage girl needs some privacy, honey, a space she can call her own."

"But we don't have the space."

"What about the attic? Could that be made into a bedroom?"

"I don't know. It's not a finished space."

"We could finish it. Put up dry wall, insulate it, put down carpet."

"What about all the boxes stored there?"

"They could be moved to the basement or the space above the garage. The attic would be better than the basement. In the basement we wouldn't be able to hear her coming and going."

"We'll talk about it later." Dale pulled into the driveway and turned off the car. "Later," he added for emphasis. He knew he had already lost.

Ashley fidgeted as she stood before her dad and stepmom. It didn't look good, seeing them sitting together on the couch.

"Sit down," her dad pointed to a chair. "We need to talk."

"What? Now what did I do?" Ashley plopped down on the chair.

"Nothing, Ash," Dale told her. "Don't worry. You're not in trouble." Ashley relaxed somewhat at this but remained guarded.

"Ava and I have been talking," Dale started.

"We realize it's hard sharing your bedroom with Grace," Ava picked up the conversation.

"So, anyway," Dale continued. "We've been talking about making the attic into a bedroom for you. What do you think?"

"Oh," Ashley thought for a moment. "I'd rather have a room above the garage."

"Out of the question," Dale responded.

"Then, okay, I guess."

"We'll fix it up. You can pick the paint and we'll get you some new furniture," Ava said.

"That is, if you want to," Dale added.

"Sure, I do," Ashley said.

"You don't sound too excited," Dale said.

"The garage would have been better, but the attic will do, or maybe the basement ..." Ashley added.

"The option is the attic or share your room with Grace." Dale began to tap his foot.

"If those are the options, I'll take the attic," Ashley said.

"There are some things we will expect you to do. Now that you are older, you can take on more responsibilities around the house —"

"—I'm already doing that, Dad," Ashley interrupted.

"And we want you to talk to Grace about your moving out. We don't want her to feel like you are abandoning her," Dale ignored the interruption.

"Sure, I'll talk to her," Ashley agreed.

"Good," Dale said, "you can go now."

"Thanks, Dad," Ashley hugged her dad then turned and hugged Ava too. "Thanks, Ava," she said before running upstairs to her bedroom.

Chapter 45

A few weeks ago, a group of people from Central America died in an over-heated truck, attempting to make it into America. What causes people to risk their lives in search of the American Dream? Surely if life were better in their own country, they would stay there.

They come to our country looking for work, willing to take jobs that most Americans are unwilling to take on, picking crops in the hot sun, working for less than minimum wage.

And what do we do? We spend money sending them back only to have them risk their lives again. And then we talk of building a wall.

I'm no expert on this, but maybe we need to be building bridges rather than walls. Or maybe we need to be spending our money on helping to correct the problems in our neighboring countries that cause them to flee, so they can stay in their own countries with their families and make a living.

It's no secret that if there were jobs available in Central American countries and lives weren't threatened every day by drug lords and gangs, there would be less people trying to escape these countries. And if employees here wouldn't hire these illegal immigrants, they wouldn't come.

So, what are we to do? I would love to hear your suggestions.

SS

"I've noticed you aren't writing your blog as often as you used to," her dad said after grace. He passed the potatoes to Marcie.

"Not as easy as it was when I could just make it up, especially with all those ideas floating by my desk each day."

"I guess it would be easier to write – what do you call it – 'fake news?'"

"Easier? Sure would. Then I wouldn't have to fact-check my writing. But it's okay. I'm learning."

"What has the response been?"

"Not good. People would rather read made-up gossip than stretch their mind and maybe learn something."

"Speaking of learning, have you given any thought to going back to school?" Henry continued to eat his supper as he raised the question, keeping his eyes on his food.

"And do what?"

"I don't care if you got a degree in underwater basket weaving. I just don't want to see all your time, not to mention my money, wasted. Would you pass the butter?"

Marcie passed the butter before responding. "It would be wasted if I go back before I know what I want to do."

"As long as you have a degree, that's your foot in the door. Employers today are more concerned about whether you are able to learn than what you have learned. They will provide the training to someone they know is teachable. The job market is changing rapidly. You have to be able to change with the market."

"That's not true of all jobs. Some still have or want basic requirements." Marcie had stopped eating as she looked at her father.

"Then get those requirements and get on with your life." Henry raised his eyes from his plate.

"Why? Are you tired of me being here?"

"Not a chance. I just hate to see you floundering so. You're like that pair of shoes hanging from the wire that you write about. One shoe on one side, another on the other side, neither planted anywhere, just dangling in the breeze. Get off the wire, make a choice, whatever that might be, then jump in with both feet."

"I do have an idea."

"Tell me."

"I was thinking about journalism. I like writing and I like exposing crime and corruption. We need good investigative reporting, delivering real news, not fake news."

"Then do it, honey."

"Only ..." her dad waited for her to continue. "Only, it will take me two more years to finish."

"So be it."

"And when I'm done, I'm thinking about international news. That means I may be traveling around the world, far from home. Even if I don't do that, there are no good jobs for reporters here in Cascade Falls."

"Marcie, I'm telling you, you need to follow your dreams, wherever they take you. I never expected you to stay in Cascade Falls forever." Henry returned to his dinner, allowing Marcie time to process what had been said before beginning again.

"I hear Bernie is leaving," Henry said.

"Yes, he has to return to Nashville to practice before going on tour."

"That's too bad."

"Really. I didn't think you liked Bernie."

"I liked Bernie. I just didn't like the situation. You okay with it?"

"Maybe we're better as just friends. Maybe we were never meant to be a couple."

"Do you really think that?" her dad stopped eating for a moment and looked over at Marcie.

"I don't know, I mean, sometimes I wonder. Wouldn't it be easier to just be friends? It seems he is always going away."

"Easier doesn't mean better." Henry finished off his plate. "You've got a good head on your shoulders, Marcie. You'll do what's right, make the best decision."

Marcie poked at her food, letting it get cold on her plate. "Dad, why did you name me Marcella? It's such an awful name."

"You think so? It was your mother's idea. The name means 'young warrior.' I think she thought you needed a fighting chance to make it in this world. As for me, I always liked the name Marcie from the Peanuts strip. She was intelligent, yet naïve. I thought maybe you'd be the best of both, a warrior when you needed to be, smart when the occasion called for it. I wasn't wrong. You have proven yourself over the summer."

"Young warrior. I kind of like that. It matters that mom chose it for me. I guess it's not so bad a name." She picked at what remained on her plate. "Dad, why didn't you ever remarry?"

"I guess one woman in my life was all I could handle."

"Come on, Dad. That's no excuse. And besides, I'll be gone soon."

"Guess the right woman hasn't come along yet. But there is that buxom brunette ..."

"Daddy!"

Henry looked over at the remaining piece of chicken. "You want that last piece of chicken?" he asked before swooping in and finishing it off.

Chapter 46

"You have a minute?" Marcie knocked on Pastor Joe's door and peeked in.

"This can't wait until our regular meeting?" Joe looked up from his computer.

"It's kind of important."

"Okay, sit down." Joe motioned to a chair as Marcie sat down.

"I've been thinking."

"Yes ..." Joe wanted Marcie to get on with it.

"I've been thinking, what do I want to do with my life? I've been thinking about going back to school."

"And ..."

"I checked and I can go back this fall." Marcie waited for his reaction. "But I don't have to. I can wait. I mean, I don't want to leave you without a secretary. I can stay until you find a replacement."

"And not go back to school this fall? Don't be ridiculous. When does school start?"

"September. I'll be around for a while. Give you time to find someone to take my place."

"I knew this was not going to be long term from the start. You would never be happy as a church secretary."

"I have enjoyed the opportunity."

"Don't lie, Marcie."

"Not at first, but I have learned a lot this summer. I've learned from you."

Joe grunted at this, waving away the compliment.

"I mean it," Marcie continued. "You don't like me much, do you?"

"You don't have to like someone to work with them." Joe tried to avoid the question. "Anything else?" he asked when Marcie didn't get up.

"Remember what you said about my grandfather? How God loves even him?"

"Yes."

"I've been thinking about that." Marcie paused. "I've decided I don't have to hate him."

"No, you don't. Hate hurts you more than the other person."

"I'm almost glad I found out about him, and about my mom, too. I appreciate who she really was, what she went through. I love her for it. The real her, not the mom I made up."

"God does work in strange ways at times."

"But I really don't know that I want to have anything to do with my grandfather."

"That's for you to decide."

"Yes, it is," Marcie stood up. "Thank you."

"For what?"

"For putting up with me, giving me a chance, you know what." Marcie continued to stand in place.

"You're welcome. Anything else?" Joe asked when Marcie didn't move.

"Oh, and I wanted to let you know, I knew what you were up to, setting me up with Ashley."

"You did? And what was that?"

"You know. I also wanted to apologize for what I wrote about you in my blog. I mean, you're a good pastor. I'm sorry if I made it seem like you weren't. I never realized all you did, all the people you helped, the difficult situations—"

"—Oh, Pastor Knowitall? But that wasn't about me, was it?"

"No, of course not." Marcie shifted her feet.

"Apology accepted. Now get out of here," Joe said, fighting the grin that was creeping across his face. He was going to miss her.

Chapter 47

"So, I guess this is it. Goodbye." Bernie turned to face her. "I hate goodbyes."

"Yet you do them so often. Seems all we ever do is say goodbye.

"You knew I had to leave come August."

"I know. Doesn't make it easier."

"Would it help if I promised to write?"

"No, don't promise what you won't do. That would make it worse."

"Dang, this is hard. It was easier to just slip away with no goodbyes." Bernie turned away.

"Is that what you want to do? Slip away like the other times?"

"You know that wasn't my choice." Bernie turned back to face her.

"Sometimes I wonder."

"Look, if you are looking for a fight ..."

"No, I'm not. Not really. We have so little time left. Let's not waste it fighting."

"We can keep in touch."

"We can, but will we? I'll be back in school. You'll be busy with your band." This time it was Marcie who turned away.

"That sounds like we are breaking up."

"Were we ever really together to start with? There's been no commitment, no promises. We knew it was just for the time we had. Fate brought us back together. Maybe fate will bring us back again."

"I don't want to leave it to fate." Bernie reached for both of her hands, forcing her to face him.

"I guess we can message each other now and then. See if our paths will cross in the future."

"That's better than saying goodbye forever."

Marcie hesitated before speaking, "So, if I'm ever in Tennessee, I'll look you up."

"You better. And if I'm ever in the area of ... where is that school of yours?"

"Northwestern, outside of Chicago." Marcie had registered for fall classes, transferring to the school of journalism.

"If I'm ever in Chicago, I'll look you up. Who knows? Maybe someday you'll be a famous reporter, travelling around the world." Bernie continued to hold onto her hands.

"And you'll be a country star, touring the nation."

"Maybe we'll meet up in some exotic locale, like Bangkok," Bernie suggested.

"Why Bangkok?"

"Don't know. It just sounded exotic. It was the first place that came to my mind."

"It's just that Bangkok is the human trafficking center of the world."

"Okay, how about Paris?"

"So cliché. What's wrong with meeting here, Cascade Falls?"

"I thought you hated it here," Bernie said.

"Yes, but it's my home, where my dad lives," Marcie was as surprised as him.

"Okay."

"Let's swear. Let's swear that in ten years ..."

"Ten years? Why ten years?" Bernie asked.

"Ten years, if our paths haven't crossed by then, we'll meet here, in Cascade Falls."

"August eighteenth here in ten years." Bernie agreed. "Only if we haven't remained in touch. Only if we drift apart. We'll meet then. I can see you as a famous reporter, traveling the world, can't you?"

"And you'll be a country star."

"I'm counting on us keeping in touch, you know. This is just a long shot, you might say. My ace in my pocket to make sure we don't lose touch forever."

"Okay. Agreed," Marcie said.

"Now we have to seal it with a kiss."

"That I can do." They kissed lightly then held each other in a last embrace. "I swear, we will dance together again," Bernie whispered in her ear before letting her go.

"Ten years, August eighteenth," Bernie said as he climbed into his truck and drove away, Blade sitting in the passenger seat. Marcie felt like a little girl again, standing in the street, watching as her friend drove out of her life once again. Who knew how long it would be this time?

"He's gone," Marcie called Gwen.

"More time for me."

"Don't start."

"I won't. I know when my friend is hurting. How about we meet for coffee? Get your mind off of him," Gwen suggested.

"Sounds perfect." Marcie hopped on her bike and rode to the Coffee Company, glancing at the tennis shoes that still dangled above as she rode by.

Chapter 48

Mysteries of the Solar System

 Today there is a complete solar eclipse. I remember there being an eclipse when I was a child. My housekeeper had me stay inside with the curtains closed lest I fail to resist the urge to look up and watch the event and end up blind. I wonder about this now. I'm surprised I haven't heard stories of people going blind after an eclipse. It would seem that if that were the case, there would be thousands or more people over the centuries who had gone blind.

 Who were the first people to look at the sun during an eclipse and go blind? There must have been somebody who then passed the message of warning on to future generations. Since this is an infrequent event, how was the message passed on through centuries and across continents, I wonder? Now there are whole groups of people, eclipse followers, who seek out this visual phenomenon.

 So many mysteries yet to be uncovered!

 I understand why primitive cultures might consider it an evil omen. If I were a time traveler, I could go back in time to the day and place of an early eclipse and pretend I was making it happen through magic. It must have been a wondrous thing to see as the sun was slowly eaten away.

 Every month the moon wanes, as if being eaten by a large monster in the sky. Then it slowly grows back. We are used to that phenomenon of the night sky, but not to losing our sun if even for but a few minutes.

 Our world is filled with so many mysteries, so many wonderful secrets, yet to be uncovered. I intend to uncover as many as I can!

           SS

"You know, I don't know if we were ever rightfully introduced." Kathleen surprised Marcie at her writing. Marcie flipped her laptop shut. Even though she now had permission to write while at work, it still felt like a guilty pleasure, one that needed to be hidden away.

"I'm Kathleen Reese," Kathleen extended her hand to Marcie.

"I know."

"I know you know." Kathleen smiled as Marcie squirmed. "Maybe you know my sons, Josh and Scott?"

"I knew of Josh. Who didn't? I watched him play football. But we went to different schools."

"Well, nice to meet you," Kathleen said and turned as if to go. Marcie started to lift the top of her laptop.

"Oh, by the way," Kathleen turned back around. "I'm a fan of your blog."

"You are?"

"Yes. I've never been referred to as a 'buxom brunette.' I've never been a 'buxom' anything."

"Well, it's fiction. I mean, what are you talking about? It's all made up."

"Is it? So, the pastor in *Delicious Secrets* isn't Pastor Joe? And he isn't secretly dating the buxom brunette?"

"Oh no, not at all. That's all made up."

"I see. If you say so." Kathleen stared intently at Marcie before turning back around.

"And besides," Marcie said to Kathleen's back. "It's no secret."

"What? What are you talking about?" Kathleen turned back around and looked at Marcie.

"You and Pastor Joe. It's no secret. Everybody knows you are dating. You aren't fooling anyone."

"Oh, they do, do they?" Kathleen pursed her lips and raised her eyebrow before continuing out the door. Marcie grinned as she flipped her laptop back open.

Chapter 49

As the summer dragged on, Ashley cut back on her visits with Pastor Joe.

"You're okay, and all, but I think I'd rather be riding my bike and playing my guitar."

"It's entirely up to you. You can come see me whenever you want, you know."

But Ashley continued to help out at the church office each Friday. She looked forward to talking to Marcie. And she continued to read Marcie's blog posts through all the changes. She had heard about what had happened at the nail salon through her dad and stepmom who had found out through her aunt Kathleen.

"What about Marcie?" Ashley had asked when she overheard them talking about her.

"Nothing for you to worry about," her dad said. "Seems she helped bring down a human trafficking network here in Cascade Falls." Ashley couldn't wait till Friday to ask Marcie about the incident but was disappointed when Edna, the former secretary, was there instead.

"Marcie is taking some time off this week," Edna had explained. "But I could use your help. I brought some of my cookies. You can have some after you're done."

When she heard that Marcie was going back to school she rode her bike to the church office rather than waiting till Friday.

"I heard you are leaving. When?" Ashley cornered Marcie in the office.

"In a few weeks."

"When were you going to tell me? What about me?" Ashley didn't wait for Marcie to answer. "It won't be any fun around here without you."

"We can still get together when I'm home from college."

Ashley thought for a moment. "That's what people always say, but they don't mean it. You'll forget about me when you're gone."

"How could I forget you? You won't let me, Miss Precocious."
Marcie smiled and tried to get Marcie to smile back at her.

"Will you still blog?" Ashley asked.

"I don't think I'll have time for it once I get back to school."
Marcie said.

"But then how will I know what you are doing?"

"I guess I could post now and then, or you could email me. Any
time, you can email me any time, about anything." Marcie wrote out
her email address and gave it to Ashley.

"I didn't like it at first, when you changed your blog," Ashley
said as she accepted the slip of paper. "But then, I saw what you were
doing and it was okay."

"Glad you liked it." Despite her not wanting Ashley's help,
Marcie had come to enjoy her company on Friday mornings, even
though it took her away from her research and writing. "Oh, and I
forgot to ask you, did my blog post help any? With the older girls, I
mean."

"No, but that's okay. They still don't talk to me. Why should I
waste my time with them?" Ashley tucked the paper in her back
pocket. "Besides, did I tell you I'm part of a band?"

"No, you didn't. That's great. Maybe I'll get to hear you play
sometime."

"And then you could write about us in your blog."

"Sure. Deal." Marcie reached across her desk and shook Ashley's
hand.

Pastor Joe walked in during the hand shake. "Hi Ashley, did we
have an appointment?"

"No, Pastor, I was just telling Marcie about my band."

"You're in a band? That's great."

"And I'm getting my own room," Ashley added.

"More good news. Sounds like this has been a big summer for
both of you." Ashley and Marcie exchanged glances, then laughed.

"More than you know," Marcie said, "but that's our secret, right
Ashley?"

Chapter 50

"It's been a good summer." Marcie turned over and sat up, wiping sand off of her swimsuit.

"I can't believe you are leaving." Gwen turned over as well, sitting up. "Bernie's gone and soon you'll be gone. Then it will just be me. What'll I do without you? How can you leave me here?"

"You don't have to stay here."

"You know I do." Marcie did know that, she didn't know why she had such a hard time remembering it, accepting it. Marcie slid down onto her back. Gwen turned over and laid on her stomach. "What ever happened to that book you were going to write?"

"I guess it got pushed to the side by everything else. I was never really serious about it."

"With all that happened this summer, I think you've got plenty material for a book."

"Maybe. But not right away. First, I have to get through college. I don't know what my dad will do if I drop out again."

"You can do it." Gwen smiled and flipped over on her back. "Write the book that is, and make it through college."

"Do you remember how your mom used to call us her princesses? Princess Marcella and Princess Gwendolyn." Marcie asked as she stared at the lids of her eyes.

"Of course. Mom always hated it when I shortened my name to Gwen. That's not a name appropriate for a princess, she used to say. But she wasn't the one who had to write it on multiple papers every day at school."

"Did you know Marcella means young warrior? My dad told me. Said my mom picked it out for me. I think when I get back to school, maybe I'll start signing my papers Marcella. Sounds more impressive than Marcie. Maybe people will pay more attention to me with a name like Marcella, young princess warrior."

"I like it. I wonder what Gwendolyn means." They lay in silence for a while, allowing the sun to spread warmth throughout their bodies. Gwen broke the silence.

"It has been a good summer. We got our nails done, met some bikers, saved some human trafficking victims. All in all, not a bad summer. Did you get all the answers to your secrets?"

"All but one. I still don't know the mystery behind the dangling tennis shoes."

"Oh," Gwen shifted awkwardly.

"Gwen, tell me. What do you know?" Marcie sat up.

"It was me." Her voice was barely audible.

"What?"

"It was me."

"You?"

"Yes, me."

Marcie took off her hat and hit Gwen with it. "Why didn't you tell me?"

"It was just a thing."

"A thing?"

"You know, one of those crazy things you do when you feel like you are going to explode. I took my shoes off, tied them together and flung them over the wire. I just wanted to see if I could do it."

"Why didn't you take them down?"

"They were old shoes. I didn't need them. And then you started fixating on them. I thought, what harm to leave them there?"

"Why didn't you tell me?"

"And ruin all of the suspense? No, I was having much more fun with them hanging there than I ever did wearing them."

Marcie paused. "You want to try and get them down? One last adventure?"

"Nah, let someone else wonder about them. I've had enough adventure for one summer."

They flipped back to their other side, soaking up the last days of summer.

"It has been a good summer," Marcie said again as she closed her eyes and basked in the feel of the sun on her back.

"What will I do without you?" Gwen said once again.

Marcie turned on her side and smiled at Gwen. "I hear there's a job opening at the church, for a secretary ..."

Farewell Post

This will be my last post, at least for a long time, which in internet terms, means farewell forever. I'll soon be forgotten as someone new comes along and claims their fifteen minutes of fame. One minute you're going viral, the next you've sunk back into the abyss of all those other bloggers and blogger wannabes, struggling to get noticed. I'm grateful you noticed me!

Thank you to those who have followed me over the past few months, especially those who stayed with me through the changes to format. Perhaps Pastor K and the Church of St. Everybody will have a resurrection in some form at a later date. Perhaps not. Perhaps it's best to leave its secrets lost in the blogosphere.

As for me, I've learned a lot this summer. I've learned that some secrets, I'd rather not know. They are best kept by the people most concerned. I've also learned a greater respect for secrets and the people who keep them, the secretaries of the world.

It seems I'm not much of a secretary. Guess I was never meant to be one. That's why I am going back to school to seek out my life's calling through the school of journalism.

I know it may seem like a strange time to enter this field. Journalists are under attack, discredited and even hated by many who blame the media for everything that's wrong with the world. Why would I want to join such a beleaguered group? It's a secret to me. I'm not sure I know myself!

I still believe there is truth out there and that we need an informed press corps to help us understand the truth about what is going on in our world. Not just blurting out opinions, but people who have the time and the integrity to seek out the truth wherever it may take them, even if it takes them into harm's way, even if it means possibly being thrown into jail.

The world needs investigative reporters more than ever. With so much information available at the touch of a screen, we need people who can help us siphon out the truth amidst all of the confusing, conflicting information. Your average person doesn't have the time to do this research. That's why they need reporters they can trust.

So, I'm going to school to become one such reporter, to learn how to discern credible information from lies, to recognize bias, my own and others, and to actively seek out information that may be contradictory to what I believe, people who may not think the same as I do, all in a search for truth.

And if I uncover some secrets in the process ... so be it! I am no longer a keeper of secrets, but a revealer of secrets!

Thank you again for following this blog. I hope you will follow me again someday when I make my debut as an investigative reporter. Until then, signing off.

SS

Note to the Reader:

Did you enjoy reading this book? If so, please leave a review on Amazon. Your comments would be appreciated and mean so much to me in terms of helping others notice my book. You, the reader, have the power to make or break a book in this day of emarketing and social media.

Thank you so much for reading *Delicious Secrets*. Stay tuned for the next book in the series, *Beautiful Questions*!

Patricia M. Robertson

Other Novels by Patricia M. Robertson

Dreamweavers – Dream again, wherever you are in your life.

Buying Time – Visit the peace movement during the Cold War era of Ronald Regan, SDI (Strategic Defense Initiative) and MAD (Mutually Assured Destruction).

Land of Deep Waters - Honduras, land of deep waters, a country torn apart by civil unrest, violence and poverty: Is it possible to go back?

Magnificent Failure - Is it possible to start over? Failures in the eyes of the world and their own eyes, Diane and Jake found each other.

Dancing Through Life Series

Dancing on a High Wire – What do you do when life knocks you off balance? Join Sara, Joy and Esther as each seeks to find a "new normal" and regain their balance on this high wire we call life.

Still Dancing - Some phone calls we love, others we hate, like the ones Pastor Joe receives from his daughter's school. Or the one Dale received at work, letting him know his wife, Joy, had fallen and was in route to the hospital by ambulance. Could her cancer be back?

A Slow Waltz - The road to healing from loss is a slow one, sometimes going backward and sideways before going forward. Sometimes the biggest barrier to healing lies within us. Join Dale, Kathleen, Ava and others as they journey to forgiveness and healing.

An Irish Slip Step -The Irish slip jig is set in 9/8 signature time, unusual and a little off balance, like life! Kathleen didn't know about the slip jig, but she knew about slipping up. It seems her life was one long slip step! As was Chloe's, whose life was knocked off balance by an unplanned pregnancy. And then there was that fiery red-head, Mary Helen, who fell in love with an American soldier.

Was it a slip-step or one of life's fortuitous missteps that brought them precisely where they were meant to be?

About the Author

Patricia M. Robertson is an author, speaker and spiritual director, who is committed to helping individuals find God in their every day experience. She also is author of a companion non-fiction book to *Still Dancing, Walking with Families through the Dying Process*, as well as *Walking with Families through Grief,* a companion to *A Slow Waltz.*

She has written other non-fiction books and writes a weekly blog and monthly newsletter. She has a Doctor of Ministry and over thirty-five years of experience in ministry to families. She currently is enjoying her own love story with her husband, Jack, grown children and grandchildren. For more information about her ministry, go to www.patriciamrobertson.com.

BEAUTIFUL QUESTIONS

Gwen sat on her hands as Pastor Joe looked over her application. Where was the easy-going smile she was used to seeing on Sundays? Instead his eyebrows crinkled, his lips remained firm in a straight line, neither going up nor down to indicate his thoughts. Did she dare break the silence?

"So," Pastor Joe sighed as he pushed the application aside and looked at her. "Why do you want to be a church secretary?"

Gwen was prepared for this question. "I've been a member of this church for most of my life. I love the church. I thought I might do some good."

"Oh," Pastor Joe's eyes bore into her as if searching out her very soul. This was a side of the pastor Gwen was not familiar with. So intense. "You and Marcie are friends."

"Best buds." Gwen wasn't sure whether this was a selling point or not. Marcie had been the previous secretary. She had left after only six months in order to go back to college.

"I don't know what Marcie told you, but it won't be like that. No time for daydreaming or playing on your computer. The church year is picking up. Sunday school is starting again, other church activities. You won't have the free time Marcie had over the summer."

"I know, Pastor. That's what I want. I'm a good worker. I'd rather be busy than bored."

"You don't have any previous work experience."

"I know but I have good references. I've done well in school." Gwen looked over at Pastor Joe. How much did he know? How much dare she tell? "I've been busy taking care of my mom."

"Yes, I'm aware of that." What would Pastor Joe do? He had taken on Marcie last spring as a favor to Marcie's dad. Gwen was aware how that had ended. Six months later and he's back looking for another secretary. He picked up her application again. "How will you fit in work with school and your family responsibilities?"

"I can take classes at night and my mom's doing much better or I wouldn't be here."

"And when do you graduate? What are you going to do after that?"

"I graduate in the spring, but I promise, I won't leave you without notice. I'll give you a month, two months' notice, before I leave, if I leave." Pastor Joe tapped his finger on the desk as he thought.

Gwen shifted up and down on her hands then broke the silence. "Please, Pastor, I really need this job. If I don't get out of that house, I'll go crazy. I'll work harder than anyone else could or would. I'll work overtime, no charge. I'll work late, weekends, whatever it takes to get the job done. Just give me a chance. I'll be the best secretary you've ever had."

Pastor Joe shook his head and looked at her application. Gwen could see the doubt in his eyes. She knew about Edna, his secretary before Marcie. Edna had been the best secretary he ever had, Gwen knew that but she was convinced that given the opportunity, she could do better. She watched him look over her application and think.

"Okay," Pastor Joe put down the paper, "I'll think about it and let you know in a day or so."

"Thank you, Pastor." Gwen stood up and reached out her hand across the desk. Joe didn't accept the offer, sending her away with a flick of his wrist.

"Wait," Pastor Joe stopped her. "You aren't a writer, are you?

"No, Pastor. I'm an actress."

Now that the interview was over, Gwen wasn't sure she wanted the job anymore. Pastor Joe had seemed so different from all of her other interactions with him. Formal, distant, demanding. Not the warm, huggable man she met each Sunday. Was it all a sham? Which was the real pastor? Now she understood Marcie's dislike of Pastor Joe at first. Marcy, if only she could talk to her best friend, but she was away at school. It was only a four-hour drive, but it might as well be light years. Marcie was moving on with her life while she was stuck here in Cascade Falls. Everyone, all of their friends from high school, had moved on, either to school or jobs in other cities. There was nothing to keep them here, no jobs, no opportunities. And here she was stuck.

Gwen noticed the pair of tennis shoes dangling from the overhead wire. Maybe she should have taken up Marcie's offer to knock them down. Over the summer it had been fun to hear Marcie wonder about why and how they had been launched to their heights. Now they seemed to taunt her. They were a reminder of how she was stuck, stuck in this town where the best job she could get was that of a church secretary and a part-time one at that.

Marcie had always been full of fun, creating adventures wherever she went. Only Marcie could make a mystery out of a pair of tennis shoes dangling from a wire. Only Marcie made her life bearable. That was why she needed this job. She needed it so she could make some money, put it aside and finally get out of here. Of course, she couldn't tell the pastor that. He would never hire her if he knew the truth. But she did mean what she had told him about working hard. She would show him. She would show everybody, if only she got the chance. Just give her a chance.

"Marcie, call me. I had the interview with Pastor Stick Up His Butt. You were right. Call me." Gwen left the message on Marcie's phone. She was probably in class, where Gwen ought to be except she had already arranged her schedule in anticipation of getting the job. She had to get it.